- *How can I recognize well-made furniture?*
- *Should I go wall-to-wall or stick with area rugs?*
- *What exactly is a "breakfront" anyway?*
- *How can I tell if I'm buying a good quality mattress?*
- *What kinds of lighting do I need to think about?*

Whether you're starting from scratch or just putting a new twist on your old decor, *Make Yourself at Home* is the perfect planning guide—filled with expert advice on everything from the basics of painting and floor planning to the special finishing touches that make your place uniquely yours—and make a house a home!

MAKE YOURSELF AT HOME

MAKE YOURSELF AT HOME

BO NILES

B

BERKLEY BOOKS, NEW YORK

MAKE YOURSELF AT HOME

A Berkley Book / published by arrangement with
the author

PRINTING HISTORY
Berkley edition / January 1995

ISBN: 0-425-14536-0

BERKLEY©
Berkley Books are published by The Berkley Publishing Group,
200 Madison Avenue, New York, New York 10016.
BERKLEY and the "B" design
are trademarks belonging to Berkley Publishing Corporation.

PRINTED IN THE UNITED STATES OF AMERICA

10 9 8 7 6 5 4 3 2 1

CONTENTS

INTRODUCTION

The Idea of Home

Although we are no longer cave dwellers, ducking in out of the rain or retreating from danger, we still regard shelter as a fundamental necessity. Besides fostering a feeling of safety and protection, just what is it about shelter that makes us feel comfortable? What makes us feel good? What makes us feel, literally, *at home?*

You know when you enter someone's house whether it feels, as Goldilocks would say, "just right" or not. When it does, you feel at home. Why? It's not just the way the furniture is arranged, although that helps. Nor does it derive only from the color scheme, although color certainly affects our mood. Nor is it merely reflected by an assembly of objects, although a person's choice of possessions reflects his or her taste and personality. It is all these things—and more. Home is more than the sum of its parts.

In practical terms, a house or apartment is designed and constructed as a composition of rooms. Each room consists of walls, windows, doors, floors, and ceilings, as well as invisible pathways from door to door, and, perhaps, distinctive built-in elements such as a fireplace, bookcases, or an alcove.

The decoration of a house is composed of embellishments, the assembly of cosmetic effects and furnishings that translate what is given—the designed rooms—into someplace personal, the place that is your own and no one else's. These embellishments comprise the paint and/or wallpaper, carpet and/or rugs, the furniture, the lighting, window dressings and bed linens, your books, paintings, or other artwork, CDs and/or videos, and all the individual and idiosyncratic things you collect just because you love them and want them close by.

A Sense of Style

Webster's dictionary defines the word *style* as a "distinctive manner of expression" or "custom of behaving," and so it is. Your personal behavior and your personal style of dress set you apart and define you as an individual.

Style is also defined as "a particular mode of living," and thus historically meant how furnishings and artifacts were arranged to reflect prevailing fashion and taste.

Until the Industrial Revolution and the advent of the machines that would allow furnishings and objects to be mass-produced, style manifested itself most obviously and spectacularly in the homes of the wealthy, ruling classes. Beautiful furnishings and decorative objects were costly; each piece of furniture and each object, such as a porcelain bowl or a crystal goblet, was crafted by hand. Through the influence of the prevailing monarchy and aristocracy, a particular style or mode of decoration persisted, in a remarkably consistent manner, for a substantial period of time, until it was supplanted by the influence of an ascendant patron.

With the Industrial Revolution, the pace accelerated and styles followed one another with increasing frequency. The potential for assuming a style became available to all, and ultimately styles overlapped, which they continue to do today.

With increased mobility and ease of travel to farther and farther points around the world, a particular style was no longer confined to a particular nation or locale, either. A style might be interpreted, then reinterpreted in a different place.

Today, anyone can affect style—or a style. With a renewed

pride of heritage and ethnicity, styles range from one based upon a particular national or historical reference to those that artfully combine many influences in an eclectic look.

Personal Style

In America, where we constantly feel the tug between individualism and conformity, or self-expression and peer approval, the very notion of style may intimidate. It doesn't have to. At heart, style is simply this, to quote Webster's dictionary once again: ''an ease of manner''—a confidence in yourself and your taste. This is me; this is where I live; this is what I love to have around me.

Style boils down to what feels right to you.

What This Book Will Do—and Not Do

What this book will **not** do is tell you what style to emulate. It only wants to help you feel comfortable with your decorating decisions.

First, we'll take a look at you for clues to what you'd like to live with. In a way, this is the most important chapter of all, because it will help—and should encourage—you to feel more confident about what you want and need to live with, if you don't feel this way already.

Next, we'll tackle the nitty-gritty of figuring out how to work with the space you have. This is a hardworking chapter that shows how to make a floor plan, and it is followed by a discussion about how to arrange the furniture in a room. How you feel about the things you own and how your furniture is arranged are the two most important indicators of comfort.

The Background and Components of Decoration

Next we'll consider the background for decoration: the ceilings, walls, and floors in your home. It is a good idea to make the background as smooth and blemish-free as possible, because then it will set off and enhance your furniture and other possessions. An ugly background will only make your belongings appear somehow dingy or insignificant.

After we establish how to make the background as attractive as possible, we'll look at fabric and at the various items that come into play in a decorating scheme: furniture, carpeting and rugs, lighting and lamps, window dressings, and, lastly, accessories.

Once we're done, you should have a good idea of what makes you feel at home.

Working with the Book

This book is set up so that you can read it through from cover to cover, following the design and decorating process from beginning to end—but you don't have to do this if you don't want to. If, for example, you feel perfectly happy with your belongings and are moving from one place to another, you may want to skip right over the first chapter to the second, or even the third, if you want to know a little more about arranging furniture. You may only want to garner some tips about specific furnishings, such as carpet or window dressings. You may want to make a floor plan, but don't really need extra advice about bed linens.

Feel free to scan the book, then wander about in it as you please. Think of it as a friend and ally. Carry it with you when you shop for a piece of upholstered furniture, for instance, or for a lampshade.

So, let's begin. Have fun. Enjoy yourself. That way you will feel comfortable about making your home feel comfortable. That way you will feel at home.

PART ONE

Devising a Floor Plan

CHAPTER 1

Looking at Yourself

You can tell when someone's home feels comfortable. Everything in every room feels as if it belongs there. There is a consistency between person and place, a harmony that evolves from design and decoration fused with a particular, intimate—and personal—expression of style and taste.

Before you decorate your place, take a close look at **yourself** for cues and clues to how you want to live and what you want to live with.

Keeping a Home Book

When you start to think about how to make yourself comfortable in your new home, buy a diary or loose-leaf notebook to use exclusively as a *home book*. A good kind is one that's easy to carry in your pocket or purse or briefcase. Even better is one that

has a holder for a pen or pencil. That way you can take notes
spontaneously and without hassle.

A Diary and a Helpmate

A home book is useful, first of all, as a datebook, for keeping
track of how your home evolves, day by day and week by week.
Why? Because you can track when you decided to purchase items
for your home, when deliveries of merchandise ordered over the
telephone are expected, when workmen are due to arrive, and
other details.

A home book is a practical helpmate when you go shopping,
so that you can record information about things you might like to
have in your home, even if these items seem beyond your budget.
Perhaps you can copy an idea you see in a store in a way that will
be less costly or less elaborate.

A home book is also useful as a journal. It's a good place to
record impressions and thoughts and feelings as they occur to you
throughout the process, from the beginning straight through to
when you move in.

Honoring Memories

Before you begin to consider exactly how you want to decorate
your house, take some time to think about what you love or loved
about places you recall from your past, and take note of places
you enjoy being in today, too. You may be surprised to see what
feelings and images this homework inspires. It is very possible
that some of these vivid, happy interior "furnishings" can be
translated into your new home.

Rooms from the Past

First, recall rooms from your past that arouse good feelings in
you. What, for instance, appealed to you about your childhood
home? What do you remember about the homes belonging to your
grandparents or other relatives or special friends?

Memory may inspire an all-pervasive feeling of warmth, perhaps, or of light. Or it can be selective. Quite often it may only
comprise a lingering, flickering image of a room, or even another
sensation altogether, such as a fragrance or a fragment of music.
We may remember only part of a room in which we were happy.

The point is to think of ways you can transport the mood into your new home.

Starting with Specifics

Maybe the feeling comes from something very specific, such as a big, comfortable, old armchair where we curled up before a fire or where we were read to as a child. Maybe it is a dinette table and chairs where we gathered for breakfast before dashing off to school.

Maybe it is the scent of freshly folded bed linens, or the aroma of a freshly baked piecrust, pulled from the cavernous maw of a big, old oven. And maybe it's just a glimmer of a ray of sun upon a bare wood floor in a musty attic where we played hide-and-seek among a horde of trunks and boxes.

Recalling Particulars

Then, zero in on aspects of your memories that are even more specific, and that you remember with affection. For example, if you remember a particular fabric from a screened-in porch of your youth or the delicious color used on your childhood bedroom furniture or the wallpaper used in your grandmother's guest bedroom, consider replicating some of these features in your new home. You do not have to copy the fabric or paint or paper precisely, but you might like to find something that brings back the same happy feelings.

If you recall the exact shape and style of a particular chair you found cozy when you were young, you may want to look for a similar chair for your new living room. If your best friend had a rug you admired in her family dining room, or a set of dishes, think about telephoning and finding out more about these so that you can seek out similar items for yourself.

Observe Your Surroundings

Next, when you visit your friends and extended family—or even people you do not know so well—take the time to observe your surroundings. Is there something special about the arrangement of the furnishings that pleases you? Is there a particular way the windows are dressed or a rug is laid before a hearth or under a table? Is there a specific piece of furniture that appeals to you, or a lamp, or a wallpaper pattern, or a way a room is painted?

Register your likes—and your dislikes as well—in your mind. Let your curiosity be your guide and ask questions about the things you love in all these places. Make notes, if you can, or mental notes that, when you have a moment, you can jot down in your home book.

Check Out Showcase Rooms

Fantasy can be indulged firsthand in model rooms created by department stores and in decorator showhouses. Showhouses, conceived and decorated to raise money for charitable organizations, are usually held in the spring or fall. The fee may seem hefty—usually about ten to fifteen dollars—but you will come away with a catalog full of resources, as well as the knowledge that you are helping a worthy cause.

Because they want to show off their creativity and drum up new business, decorators tend to pull out all the stops in their showcase rooms. There is no actual client involved in a showhouse, of course, so decorators often take the opportunity to experiment with materials and new ideas—ideas that you can take note of, along with their resource lists in the showhouse catalog.

Making a Wish List

Fantasy is a wonderful ally in the quest for what makes you feel at home. A dream or wish list often leads to wonderful, original ideas that can be adjusted to meet your budget.

Take advantage of every opportunity to explore and to learn about what's going on in the decorating world, even if it seems rather highfalutin or out of reach. If you have never done so before, look more closely at the rooms and houses featured in the movies and on television.

When you are at your local newsstand, flip through or buy some of the so-called "shelter" or decorating magazines that make a point of featuring pretty rooms and/or well-designed houses. Some of these magazines zero in on particular aspects of design from time to time, too; they may occasionally devote a special section to window treatments, for instance, or to paint techniques, or to wallpapering.

Look over your newsstand for special-interest publications if you want to learn more about a particular subject such as weekend decorating or remodeling projects or country-style decorating ideas. Finally, don't forget to check out the special style sections that run periodically in newspapers.

Start a Clip File

Start a clip file to go along with your home book. An accordion file is perfect because you can divide up your clippings pocket by pocket. Dedicate one pocket to each room, and keep separate pockets for the exterior of your house, if this applies, and for your lawn or garden. When a photograph of a room or detail within a room catches your fancy in a magazine (or newspaper), cut it out and place it in your file.

If you want to keep track of specific information pertaining to particular items in a photographed room, look up the feature by its title and page number in the product information section at the back of the magazine, and check to see if the items you are interested in are described there. If so, clip the relevant page and staple it to its counterpart for future reference. Some magazines alphabetize the addresses of the manufacturers featured in their stories in a separate listing; you may want to clip this listing as well and highlight the addresses relevant to your photographed room.

Make Photocopies

If you do not want to purchase any of the magazines you find and you do not mind black-and-white representations, you can photocopy the pages that interest you from the magazines carried in the periodicals section of your local library.

While you are in the library, don't overlook the section devoted to home design and lifestyle. When you persue a book and turn to rooms you like, photocopy these, too. Some of the home/lifestyle books include comprehensive resource directories at their conclusion; you may want to photocopy these as well to aid you in your search for specific items that are not obtainable in your hometown.

A Pattern Emerges

As you begin to compile your notes in your home book and assemble clippings in an accordion file, you should find a pattern
emerging that reflects a sense of what you like.

Take out your clippings and spread them out on a table or the
floor. What is consistent about the rooms you clipped? Are there
elements or facets of a room that repeat themselves over and over?
A color palette, for example? The way the furniture in the rooms
is arranged? A window treatment? Or just a mood?

In the following chapters, we will translate these patterns of
what appeals to you most in your fantasies, notes, and clippings
into a home you will feel comfortable in and will love.

One Major Clue: How You Dress

How do you dress and present yourself to your family, friends,
and colleagues? Because we are taught how to dress ourselves
long before we are given a chance to dress up a room or a whole
house or apartment, we have practice in pulling together colors
and outfits that make us feel good, and in terms of being out in
the world, at home with ourselves. By the time you are ready to
engage in ''dressing'' or decorating a place of your own, you
probably will have tried out and shed myriad clothing ''personalities'' to arrive at a look that's distinctly you.

Styles of Clothing

What style of clothing feels best to you? Romantic, tailored, clas-
sic, exotic, casual? Are you consistent in your approach to your
clothing choices, or do you like to dress up and down and experiment with different types of clothing to enhance a particular
event or mood?

Some people, of course, dress for public in a manner altogether
different from the way they live; many fashion designers, for
instance, who work with lots of patterns and colors during the
day, often opt for monochromatic clothing and a soothing, neutral
setting in which to relax at home. On the other hand, some people
like to turn their home space into a ''theater for living'' where
they transform their ''scene'' almost as often as their outfits.

Color and Personality

Colors have been equated with moods, and studies show that different personality types lean to specific color combinations. Outgoing, assertive persons seem to favor pure, undiluted, and often bold colors such as lipstick reds, apple greens, and bright oranges; introspective dreamers are drawn to grays or muted tones such as sage, blush, or lilac; dramatic dressers often choose an all-black wardrobe, accented with metallics, especially silver or chrome.

Colors Keyed to Seasons

Some New Age studies have keyed color personalities to the seasons. In these analyses, the hue-to-season equation is as follows: Bracing/winter = grayed or cool hues; gentle/spring = pale to sunny romantic hues; radiant/summer = bright and vivid hues; and subdued/autumn = deep, shadowed hues. In other words, an outgoing personality would be classified as a summer type, the dreamer as a spring person.

In the 1990s, colors are clear and well-defined in their intensity and tonality. You may prefer pale over punchy, a tint that is barely perceptible to the eye to one that is fully saturated, but, either way, you will find that the color or hue itself is sharp and distinct these days, not murky or drab.

The Color "Rainbow"

Every color in existence is based upon the six "rainbow" hues. The six consist of three undiluted primaries—red, yellow, and blue—and their complementaries, or paired blends—orange (red and yellow), green (yellow and blue), and purple (blue and red). Colors then shift gradually in tone, or intensity, with the addition of white, to make them paler, or black, to darken them.

Color Families

Take a look at the following clusters of colors. Which apply to your taste in clothing? Do you get the feeling that the same grouping(s) will complement the way you want to decorate? Think about it.

Natural/earth tones	brown, rust, burnt sienna, russet, ochre, gold, khaki, olive
Desert/dusty tones	sand, shell, blush, rose, sage, taupe, slate blue
Romantic/pale pastels	lilac, lavender, pale pink, coral, aqua, sky, celadon, seafoam green, celery, ivory, ecru
Tropical/hot pastels	hot pink, turquoise, tangerine, lemon, lipstick red, royal blue
Exotic/vivid brights	magenta, chartreuse, purple, apple green, lapis lazuli
Tapestry/jewel tones	maroon, cranberry, teal, amber, navy blue, deep purple
Antique/grayed tones	barn red, smoky blue, mustard
Monochromes	black, white
Neutrals	beige, gray

Color Feelings

You can see from the way the colors are grouped above that some of them naturally invite a warm and cozy feeling, while others appear more open and airy. In other words, a cheerful lipstick red or orange will appear to embrace you in a warm glow and a pale, watery aqua or celadon will seem more restful.

Which mood do you prefer? Does this mood resonate with the mood you inspire and enjoy in your choice of clothing? Remember, you will ultimately feel more comfortable in your home if you keep both moods in mind when you go out to choose paint, fabrics, and wall coverings for your decorating scheme.

Looking at Color Chips

There are literally thousands and thousands of colors to choose from. Go into any paint store or home center and you will find hundreds of bookmark-size cards—or paint chips—on display. These are organized by manufacturer; in other words, each paint company prints up its own range of colors on a set of cards. This is done for a practical reason; the paint store or home center cannot stock cans of every color. The color you want must be mixed. Each individual color is based on mixing percentages of true color/s (red, blue, yellow, black) with white. Colors are clustered, four to six to a card, in increments traversing a scale from light to dark. The card has a set of codes written on the back, which tell the store how to mix the colors featured on the front.

We will talk more about color in the chapter on painting ceilings and walls. In the meantime, though, paint chips, which you can take away by the handful, offer more clues to mood. Play with them to find out how colors can complement or offset each other.

If you want to consider many colors before making a final selection, you may request a fan deck. This is a narrow book that displays all the color chips offered by a particular paint company. The book opens up from one end, like a fan, so you can see all the colors at once.

Some oft-requested groups of colors, such as whites, are printed on folders. These are free for the asking, and are often set out in display racks so you can take them away without consulting a salesperson.

Dominant and Accent Colors
You may find that you are drawn to a particular color or color group over and over. At the same time, you may feel partial to another, completely different color or group of colors in a less intense way.

Think of these as dominant and accent colors.

Are the dominant colors the same as those you wear the most, too? Or are they just colors that, instinctively, make you feel comfortable?

Take Time to Consider Colors
Because color is key, both to your personality and to a decorating scheme, it's a good idea to linger as long as you can over the colors you like, much as you would over the taste of a recipe or the fragrance of a perfume. You will feel more confident about your choices if you don't react hastily. Trust your instinct and then temper it with reflection.

Your Given Possessions

Chances are you will not be starting out completely fresh when you move in and/or decorate your home. Even if this is your very first place, you probably have collected an assortment of furnishings from your childhood room, college dorm, grandmother's attic, or other sources. These are the *givens*.

Taking Stock of What You Own
What do you plan to do about these things? Keep them all? Edit and toss? Now is the time to take stock of what you own and

decide what you truly cannot live without. You may find that you are holding onto something for no particular reason other than "Well, I've had it all along." This same object may be invested with a great deal of sentimental value and you cannot bear to part with it. Especially if you are starting out, a particular piece of furniture might be what you must live with until you can afford a replacement or you can upgrade.

Rituals and Routines

How you go about your day will also affect how you plan and decorate your home. Are you an early bird or a night owl? If so, you may need to set aside a place where you can go about your business without disturbing the others in your household.

Do you entertain often, and formally? Then you may definitely want to have a dining room that is separate and apart from the rest of your living areas.

Do you spend a significant amount of time grooming? If you share your bed and bathroom with another, then you may want to plan on two separate vanities in the bathroom, or set up a dressing table for yourself in the bedroom, if there's space.

Make Everyone Feel at Home

This leads to an important issue. In order to make yourself at home, you have to be sure everyone else feels at home, too. Family members, if any, should be consulted on design and decorating schemes, both for their own rooms and for the spaces you share.

Even though this is your home, other relatives, guests, and friends should be made to feel comfortable as well when they come to visit. Make sure you have plenty of seating, for instance, even if this means simply keeping a couple of footstools at hand for easygoing friends or a stiff-backed chair for an elderly relative who may have difficulty getting up out of a deep sofa.

Public Versus Private

The issues that inspire most debate in setting up a home are those that concern privacy. Traditionally, houses were neatly divided in two: into private and public zones. Today, as our homes have become more and more compact, rooms are not regimented by function as they were at the turn of the century.

In newer homes, many architects and builders devise rooms as multipurpose spaces, allotting certain areas within them to specific activities. Thus a kitchen may include a breakfast area or dining area and even a home office, and a living room may double as an entertainment center, or a den may serve both as a study and guest room.

Where Things Happen

Where do you like to do certain things? Where, for instance, do you prefer to relax? Where do you like to read, to watch TV, listen to music? Where do you want to entertain family and friends? Where would children complete their homework?

If you like to spend some time alone, away from the hubbub, you may want to reserve one particular place all to yourself, even if it is just a cozy chair tucked away in a corner of a room. If you require a home office, you will want to set aside an area where you can work without distractions. Do you want to be able to shut a door on an unfinished project, or can you leave your work out in the open without it bothering anyone?

Do you need space for an exercise routine, or for exercise equipment? Do you need a place to set up a hobby or craft?

And, most important, where and when do you like to relax when you are alone? On the sofa; in a favorite chair; in bed; in the bathtub?

Considering Privacy

If you like, read through the individual entries in the little chart that follows, and see which pertain to you. Focus on those that reflect your personal desires. Decide which take priority and which don't matter at all to you. In tallying your responses, you will learn which areas of your house mean more to you than other areas.

Others in your family, if you are sharing your home, can follow suit. Compare notes afterward, and discuss how to make compromises so that everyone will feel comfortable.

The words *private* and *public* are added to the chart because different activities mean something different to each one of us. Some people might consider watching TV or listening to music, for example, to be a form of entertainment for a crowd, but it may be a solitary activity for another—or, it may be something that can be shared some of the time and private at other times.

                                        PRIVATE   PUBLIC

Relaxing
    Conversing
    Watching TV
    Renting videos
    Listening to music
    Playing cards
    Other

Reading
    Newspapers
    Tabloids
    Periodicals
    Books, hardcover
    Books, paperback

Collating Collections

Another issue that can cause friction is the display of possessions. How—and where—do you want to show off artwork and/or photographs? Where do you want to keep your books, CDs, tapes, and videos? Does everyone have a personal collection or hobby that must be respected and accommodated?

Some collections gravitate naturally to obvious perches; a child's family of stuffed toys, for example, nestles happily on a bed or bedroom shelves. An array of favorite teapots or set of dishes is appropriately housed in a kitchen or in a cupboard in a dining room. But what about those things that defy definition or straddle boundaries, such as a collection of high school trophies or ribbons garnered at horse shows or 4-H Club or county fairs when you were a child? What about old photographs? Old books? Souvenirs from trips? Sentimental belongings inherited from relatives?

Evaluating Collections

Look through the list that follows and focus on what you want to do with objects you love. If you are sharing your home, should some items be put away for now, for safekeeping? Discuss each group of objects that each of you brings to this new home. One person's collection is another's clutter.

You don't want to hurt someone else's feelings, but you do want your home to be comfortable and easy to take care of.

CONSIDERING COLLECTIONS

Artwork
Family photos
Family albums
Trophies and/or memorabilia
Sports equipment
Books
CDs and/or tapes
Videos
Souvenirs
Pottery or other collectibles
Other

Entertaining Encounters

Some people enjoy entertaining squadrons of friends and acquaintances at every convenient moment, while others prefer the company of a few close friends only upon occasion. Some, of course, vary between the two extremes.

Look through the types of gatherings that follow and see which pertain to your entertaining style. As you can tell, you need very little space to entertain one on one, more space if you prefer large parties. Space, of course, can be made by moving furniture out of a room. Decide what is convenient for you, and plan accordingly.

CONSIDERING ENTERTAINING	WHERE	HOW OFTEN
Tête-à-têtes		
Sit-down dinners		
Casual or impromptu gatherings		
Cocktail parties		
Barbecues		
Picnics		
Brunches		
Coffee klatches		
Teas		
Other		

Entertaining: When and Where

How and where you want to entertain will dictate how your furniture is arranged in your public rooms. Do you like to gather your friends around you as you cook, or do you keep your cooking (and serving) separate from dining altogether?

If you like to hold sit-down dinners, do you have enough space for a table to be set up permanently? Or must you pull a table, such as a drop-leaf, from somewhere else? Where will you keep your chairs? Do you linger over coffee at the table, or do you move on back into the living room after the meal is over?

Do you set out meals buffet-style, even for small groups of friends? Where will they sit? On the floor? How often, if ever, do you give large parties?

Pets and Plants

If you are going to share your quarters with a dog or cat, gerbils, hamsters, or other caged rodents, birds, or fish, or with potted plants or trees, you will have to consider how and where these are housed and cared for. Where will you place a kitty litter pan? Where will the gerbil/hamster cage or fish tank reside? Where will you store pet food? How will plants be watered or misted? Will you need an area with increased humidity (or extra/less sunlight) to maintain plant health and equilibrium?

Understanding Yourself and Your Space

Reflecting upon some or all of the above questions about yourself, you should arrive at a keener understanding of what you might want in your new home and how you will feel more comfortable there.

If you are using a home book and have jotted down your reactions to the items outlined in the little charts above, you may want to study them more in depth at this point. What impresses you about your reactions? How do you feel?

The next step is to evaluate the actual space you have to work with. There are tricks of the trade that will help you figure out where you can put everything you want and still have space to spare. In the next chapter, we'll deal with space.

To Recap

- A home book is a useful tool; as a diary or journal, it will consolidate your feelings about how you want to live, and as a helpmate, it keeps track of what you do and what you buy to make your new home work for you.
- Recalling rooms and furnishings you loved as a child may inspire room plans and decorating schemes for your new home.
- Make note of room schemes and furnishings you like and those you dislike in houses of family, friends, and others. Look at rooms in magazines and department stores or decorator showhouse rooms.
- Let fantasy be your ally; with adjustments, a wish list can be translated into reality.
- Keeping a clip file will help you make informed decorating decisions.
- Your dress style, be it romantic or tailored, may be translated into a similar home style that reflects your personality.
- Colors—especially seasonal hues—are cues to personality. One favorite color usually dominates; the rest are used as accents. The combination of colors you choose will be the basis for your decorating scheme.
- How you organize your day will impact on how your rooms should be arranged. How much time you'd like to spend alone or with others will influence your design scheme.
- Plan enough storage and display space ahead of time, so you can showcase your favorite things.
- Don't forget pets and plants.

CHAPTER 2

Planning Your Space

A house or apartment is really just a series of interrelated boxes. Each box, or room, comprises six sides, or surfaces: four walls, a ceiling, and a floor. The walls are pierced by windows and doors. They may be embellished with architectural detail.

When we move into a place, we tend to take the rooms for granted. In other words, we usually don't question their design, unless we are actively involved in their construction or remodeling. How the rooms appear, how they are interconnected, and their size all affect how we feel about them, though, whether or not we are consciously aware of it.

Moving In

When most people move into a place, they tend to have their movers set down their furnishings here and there in a way that's convenient and works fine at that moment, and then they wonder later why they do not feel at home. They resign themselves to their situation, believing it to be unredeemable. If they feel motivated, perhaps they move a few things around, but don't quite get it right—or so they feel.

Why? Because, before you consider the decoration of your home, you must understand its underpinnings. Your place is defined and outlined by its architecture, its design. Here we will explore the various facets of design and then find out how to create a good floor plan as the backdrop for your decoration.

Considering Space and Light

What made you decide to live in this particular place rather than in another?

When you look around for a place to live, you rely both on common sense and instinct. Your common sense evaluates your choice of home in terms of its location (Is it convenient to your job, to children's schools, and to favorite activities?) while your instinct, your gut reaction, lets you know, deep inside, if you have good vibes about the place.

It is hard to describe vibes, but you know them when you feel them. Typically, vibes reveal how a space feels. Space, in turn, is affected by light. For many people, a bright space gives off happy vibes. A dark space often gives off gloomy ones. To some people, though, a dark space feels cozy.

Looking at Empty Space

When you first move into a place—or even before, if possible— try and spend some time in it when it is completely empty, for your first consideration, before placing a single piece of furniture or selecting a paint color, should be: How do you feel about your home in terms of its space and its light? Think of this as you might when you try on clothes for size. How does each room fit? Does each room "hang" well around you?

Do you like the size of every room? Do you like how the rooms relate to each other? Can you move easily from one room or area to the next, and to the outdoors, if this applies?

What is the orientation of each room to the path of the sun?

Which areas get sun in the morning and which in the afternoon? Do you have views? A yard? Neighbors nearby?

Altered States

All of these factors affect your instinctive reaction to and subliminal perception of where you live. You will want the design and decoration of your home to enhance the positive aspects of the space, and play down its negatives, so that your gut feelings about your place will be good—and will stay good. You want to reinforce a sensation of comfort and well-being, for yourself and for everyone who comes into your home.

How can you do this?

Drawing Up a Floor Plan

First and foremost, you have to devise a good design scheme for your space. For the purposes of decorating your home and making it feel comfortable, the design is, in essence, a floor plan. It takes the three-dimensional structure, proportion, and shape of a room and, translating it to a two-dimensional plan, relates the furnishings to it.

Without a floor plan, your furnishings may appear to be thrown together at random. A floor plan will illustrate how furniture can be arranged and it visually describes the traffic patterns, or invisible pathways, that are established between the furnishings as well as the pathways you travel as you move from room to room. A floor plan is also helpful when you want to figure out the placement of lighting.

A Valuable Effort

If you are not already certain about how you want to arrange your personal possessions, creating a floor plan makes sense. Creating a floor plan takes a little time, but the effort repays itself many times over. Not only do you establish a design scheme, but you can also avoid costly mistakes, such as purchasing a piece of furniture—an extra-plump sofa, for example, or an armoire—that might not fit through a standard doorway or turn the corner in a stairwell.

Preplanned Rooms

You do not need to make a detailed floor plan of every single room, but **only** the rooms that must accommodate complex furniture arrangements. Don't feel that you are being lazy if you decide you don't want to make a plan of every room—or even of any room. Your kitchen and baths, for example, are probably already designed for you, and a guest room, if you have one, or a baby's room, may require only a minimum of furnishings when you first move in.

In other words, make it easy on yourself. Only spend time on a room that may cause confusion, or that has more than one design option. In some cases, a room may actually tell **you** what to do; if it is broken up by lots of windows and doors, or it has a huge fireplace or lots of built-in bookcases, you may have to place your furniture in a certain way to avoid bumping into these elements.

Making a Rough Sketch

Before making a real floor plan, though, it is best to sketch out a rough outline of the room. All a sketch does is establish the basic outline of the room. Once the outline is determined, you can visualize the amount of floor space you have to work with and the obstacles you have to avoid.

Sketching an Empty Room or a Furnished One

A rough sketch or outline of a room, and a more formal floor plan obviously are easier to measure out and draw when a room is empty, and so, as stated above, it is a good idea to try to do so **before** you move in. It is easier to visualize a space when it is empty. It is easier to experiment with furniture arrangements on paper; big pieces of furniture are difficult to move once they are set in place.

Doodling is Essential

An outline is helpful because you can doodle on it without feeling you will make an irreversible mistake. Make lots of photocopies first, so you won't have to erase any of your ideas.

The final floor plan takes off from the most complete and comfortable version of your rough sketch and elaborates upon it so that you will have an accurate rendering of every element within the room, including your ideal furniture arrangement.

A Quadruled Pad

All you need to draft or set up a first rough sketch and the final floor plan as well is gridded—or quadruled—paper, which is available in single sheets or in pads at an art supply store. The grid is printed in pale blue on white. This blue is an easy color to work with as a background because it does not intrude upon or conflict with penciled lines.

The quadruled paper to ask for is one that is measured out so that four squares equal one inch; this configuration conforms to the standard scale of ¼" = 1'. This is the ratio most often used by designers and architects when they draw up house plans for clients.

You can find sheets of quadruled paper that are as big as 24" × 36", but pads usually come in the more commonplace 8½" × 11" format. This format converts to thirty-four squares wide by forty-four squares long, which is more than big enough to fit in a typical room; (few of us live in 34' × 44' rooms!)

Other Necessary Tools

You will also need an 18"-long straight-edge (preferably steel) ruler; a small plastic see-through, right-angle (45-45-90) triangle; and sharp, easy-to-erase number 2 or 2H pencils with erasers.

If you are feeling especially diligent, you might want to purchase an architect's scale and a T-square, too. An architect's scale is a 12"-long triangular ruler that displays a variety of different scales (such as ¼" = 1'; ½" = 1') on each of its three sides. Markings pertaining to each scale tell you instantly how many units equal how many feet. This is handy if you want to draw a plan that does not conform to the ¼" = 1' rule.

Made of steel or wood and plastic, a T-square does, indeed, look like a T; it forms a right angle between the edge and across the paper. A T-square is good for drawing straight horizontal lines across the paper. It also functions as a secure base, or resting point, when you use a triangle to draw exact vertical lines.

You will also need a thick, strong tape measure or a wooden folding carpenter's rule to calculate the actual measurements of each room. You can purchase both of these in your local hardware store or home center.

A Separate Notepad and Pencil

You will also need a pad and pencil to jot down all your measurements and to make notes about any peculiarities in the room. You can keep this list separate in your accordion file, as an extra point of reference.

Measuring Walls for the Sketch

The primary function of the rough sketch is to establish an outline of the basic dimensions of a room. How long is each wall? How many square feet are contained within the space overall? It is easy to figure these out. Start in one corner of the room you will be sketching and run your rule or tape measure along the wall at the junction of the floor and wall until you reach the next corner of the room. Write down this measurement on your notepad.

Inches and Feet

Because a tape measure or carpenter's rule is marked in inches, it is easiest to first calculate each measurement in inches. Once you know the overall length of a wall in inches, you can divide it by twelve to figure out its length in feet. Jot both figures on your notepad.

At this point, do not worry about the thickness of a baseboard, even if this will add an inch or two to the perimeter of the room. For the moment, you can also disregard any obstructions, such as a jog in the corner (the protrusion that usually hides the heating pipe and/or other utility lines) or any other idiosyncratic architectural element. Remember, this is only a rough sketch. Repeat the process for each wall.

Roughing in the Outline

Once you have all your basic measurements in hand, roughly draw the outline of the room onto your quadruled paper, allowing one square (that is, ¼", as mentioned above) for each foot. Can you now begin to visualize the shape and outline of the room?

If the length of a wall is fractional—that is, it does not come

out to an even foot—draw your line across, stop, and mark the
last square at the approximate point where the wall would end.
In other words, if a wall is 12' 6" long, then you would draw your
line only halfway across the thirteenth square.

(If your room is quite small, you may prefer to double the
quadrule ratio and work with $\frac{1}{2}" = 1'$, or two squares per foot.)

Developing the Sketch

Next, remeasure each wall, but only up to an obstruction (such
as a jog in the wall or the edge of a built-in bookcase) or to an
opening (a window or a door). Jot down this measurement, then
continue across the obstruction or opening. How wide is this feature? Jot down this figure, too.

As you cross each obstruction or opening, stop and position it
on your roughly sketched silhouette of the room. Mark the outsides
of each opening or obstruction with a little line. Continue around
the perimeter of the room until you have located and marked every
break in the walls.

Keep your calculations at hand so that they can be trasnferred
to the final floor plan; it is a good idea to jot them down on the
rough sketch, too, for easy reference.

Making a Final Floor Plan

The final floor plan evolves from the rough sketch. Your rough
sketch, of course, provides the outline of the basic perimeter of
the room, but you must remeasure all your dimensions this time
to within a quarter of an inch so that you will come up with the
accurate boundaries of the space.

Accuracy Matters

Why do you need to be so precise? Because many elements of a
decorating scheme rely on accurate measurements. Wall coverings, for instance, must be matched across their seams. A piece
of furniture might have to fit through a doorway, turn a corner in
a stairwell, or be sandwiched between two windows, bookcases,
or a bed, or it might have to be inserted into an alcove.

Architects and designers measure even more precisely than you
have to—to within $\frac{1}{16}"$ or even $\frac{1}{32}"$. Custom cabinetry, for in-

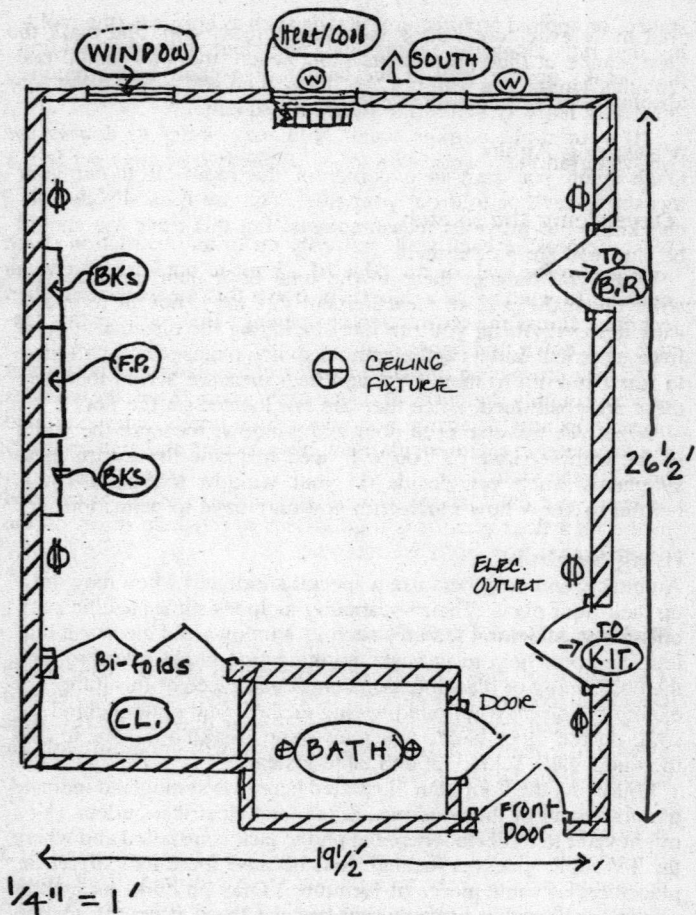

A Basic Floor Plan

stance, or applied architectural details such as cornices (the molding that runs along the ceiling line) and chair rails (the molding that breaks up the wall at the height of a chair back) require absolutely precise measurements.

Measuring Again

Once again you start in a corner of the room. Roll out your measuring tape or fold out your rule. You are basically double-checking your previous measurements, but this time you should be sure you are on the mark.

When you transfer these to the final floor plan, be sure you write down the precise measurement this time, not an estimate. Measure **everything** you run into, including the distances to and from electrical outlets and electrical switch plates. (You will have to run a rule up to their level and then measure across to where these are positioned, since they are not located on the floor).

When you traverse each door and window, measure the width of the trim separately. You will need to know these trim measurements when you decide on your window treatments. It is helpful to know how much trim you may have to paint, too.

Using Symbols

Architects and designers use a special shorthand when they draw up their floor plans. Their vocabulary includes some specific symbols for architectural features such as windows and electrical outlets. Symbols help to indicate anything that might interfere with the positioning or placement of a particular piece of furniture. For example, you may not mind having an electrical outlet behind the sofa; on the other hand, you may want to shift the sofa so that the outlet falls behind an end table instead.

Following the floor plan illustrated here, use symbols to indicate the placement of the windows, doors, and electrical outlets. (You might want to indicate where the phone jack is installed and where the TV cable access is located, too, because these may affect the placement of some pieces of furniture.) Draw in built-ins such as a fireplace or niches or bookcases because these affect the amount of usable wall space you have.

Make Photocopies

When the augmented outline of the floor plan is complete, make photocopies so that you can try out furniture arrangements on the plan. You should feel free to experiment as much as you wish. Even at this stage, doodling remains an essential part of the decorating process.

Don't forget to give every person in your household some copies of the plans, too, to get their input and ideas. You may be surprised to find out what everyone comes up with. Brainstorming a room is fun and may result in solutions no one would have thought of alone.

Photographing Your Space

Once you have your floor plans in hand, you may want to further document your rooms to clarify your ideas about each of them as a three-dimensional space. A floor plan, after all, is just that: a plan of what sits where upon the floor. It is a two-dimensional illustration of where your furniture may be placed.

Because a picture really is worth a thousand words, a photograph will tell you more about the **background** for your furniture than any floor plan can. Photographs will clue you in to how your furnishings may relate to the walls and to any built-in features such as a fireplace or bookcases.

Making Panoramas of the Walls

You do not need a fancy camera to take pictures of the walls; any camera will work, even one that takes instant exposures. What you want to do is make a sequence of shots, running around the four walls of the room. Back away as far as you can so that you can get as much of the wall in, from ceiling to floor, as possible.

Once your photos are developed, tape them together to create a panorama of each wall. Paste each "wall" on its own sheet of paper. For stability, it's best to use thick drawing paper. Leave a wide margin all around so that you can jot down any observations about how the wall looks, plus relevant measurements.

Working with a Photo Wall

A photo wall will be useful for several reasons, besides as a document for picturing your furniture in a room.

You need to know the dimensions of each wall in a room before you begin to decorate. Wall covering and paint requirements, for example, are calculated on the basis of square feet, so you need to know the height and width of each wall.

The height of a window tells you how much yardage to order for curtains or draperies, if you want to sew them yourself or have them made; you need to know the height of the window anyway, even if you buy a store-bought window treatment. The height of the window and its inside (or outside) dimension will let you know what size prefabricated curtain, shade, blind, or shutters you will have to look for.

Putting It All Together

With a rough sketch and final floor plan, plus photos of your space, you are ready to take what you now know about your space and expand upon your design scheme. Working with your floor plans, you will see how the furniture you have and the furniture you want to buy will fit into that space. In the next chapter we will look at templates, which are miniature models of furniture, to see how they can be moved around on a floor plan to create a comfortable furniture arrangement.

To Recap

- Understanding empty space and how light enters that space will offer clues about your new home's vibes and how you feel about each room.
- Walk around your empty rooms and see how they relate to each other before you move in, if possible, because you can then get a feel for what you may want to put in each room ahead of time.
- Make rough sketches of any room that might seem difficult to furnish to get a general idea of how much space you have to work with as you decorate.
- Follow rough sketches with finished floor plans so you can experiment with different kinds of furniture arrangements.
- Take accurate measurements of every architectural feature in each room, including windows, doors, and any built-ins, such as a fireplace, so that you will be sure that everything you want to place against the walls will fit.

- Make lots of photocopies and let everybody who will be sharing your new home try out design schemes.
- Photograph your rooms so you can visualize them more easily, both as a backdrop for your furniture and in order to figure out how you may want to decorate the walls and windows.

CHAPTER 3

Arranging Your Furniture

Although we will discuss specific types of furniture in later chapters, it is fun—and important—to think about the principles of furniture arrangement while you are still playing with your floor plan. You may find that you need fewer pieces than you originally thought, or you might need more. With a specific arrangement in mind, you can budget accordingly for any new furniture purchases.

Fit Before Fabric

Fabric and paint (and/or paper) are critical to a decorating scheme and ultimately serve the furniture arrangement. It is a good idea, however, to get a feeling for how you might like your furniture to fit in a room **before** you become involved in the rest of the decorating process. This will save you money in the long run, especially if you are planning to invest in new upholstered furniture. Depending upon the fabric you select, upholstery can be expensive, so it is a good idea to figure out what upholstered pieces you need—and want—to feel comfortable.

Working with Templates

One way to figure out your furniture needs is to work with templates on a floor plan. Templates are stencillike silhouettes of basic furnishings. You can find small green plastic template cards at your art supply store.

The reason to work with templates at all is that it is much easier and more efficient to shift the position of templates on a floor plan than to shove actual pieces of furniture around a room. Some pieces of furniture, notably sofas and beds, are heavy and cumbersome and you undoubtedly will want to put them in the right place right away.

The Scaled Sheet of Templates

The most common template sheet—the #111P1—is based on the $\frac{1}{4}'' = 1'$ ratio you used to draw up your floor plan. The sheet includes stencils of forty different furniture shapes, including several chairs and tables, a love seat/sofa, beds, and a couple of special pieces, such as a hutch and two styles of piano. The true dimensions of each are marked on the sheet, too.

You can also purchase templates that illustrate simple geometric shapes such as circles and squares. These can be helpful if you own a circular table, for example, or barstools.

Double-Checking Furniture You Already Own

If you already own some specific pieces of furniture, double-check their measurements to see how closely they conform to the templates. For example, if you own a wing chair, it may not match the one indicated on the template. If the measurements are close enough, it won't matter, but if they are way off, it may. Antiques or custom-made pieces exhibit a unique shape; take these into account, too.

Making Mini Furnishings from the Templates

Once you decide on the furniture you want to put in your arrangement, create your own mini pieces of furniture to move around your floor plan. This is easy to do. Trace outlines of the templates you want onto a thick sheet of paper or cardboard. Cut out the shapes.

Don't forget to make as many minis as you need. If you have a set of matching chairs, for example, you'll need to cut out a full set. Make some extra minis, too, if you are planning to add some furnishings you don't already have.

Making Minis from Scratch

If you can't find a template sheet, you can create your own minis from scratch. First, measure each piece of furniture you want to use in your arrangement. Reduce its dimensions to the scale of $\frac{1}{4}'' = 1'$. Draw an outline of the reduced piece on a sheet of heavy paper or thin cardboard. Cut out the shape.

Be easy on yourself. You don't have to make an exact replica, only an approximate one.

Keeping Track of Minis

Store minis in an envelope so that you won't lose them. Place the envelope in the appropriate room pocket in your accordion file. If you want to design furniture arrangements for more than one room, make separate sets of minis for each.

Playing with the Plan

Minis will help you decide what furniture you need in each room. You can try out an armoire, for instance, before you decide whether or not to buy one.

You can figure out what size a particular piece must be to fit in a particular situation, too. The most commonly purchased love seats, for example, are 54″ or 60″ long. Sofas start at 72″ in length; the most popular sizes are 84″ and 96″.

You can see, therefore, that you can play with minis as stand-ins both for real and hypothetical furnishings. This will help you avoid making mistakes when you purchase new furniture, and it will tell you if you must discard something you already own if it is the incorrect size or shape for the room.

Rules of the Arranging Game

When people move into a place, they often simply shove all their furniture up against the walls in each room. This, of course, frees up the center of a room, but it can be off-putting to people. Think instead of creating smaller circles or cozy zones within the room. Circles, especially circles of seating, encourage friendly exchange and conversation; they welcome.

The closer you can bring people together (without crushing them) be it in a seating circle in a living room or a family room, or around a dining table, the friendlier the mood that results. The room, or zone within the room, will feel more comfortable, too.

The Living Room, for Example

In the living room, it makes sense to place a sofa up against the longest wall, but, if you have a fireplace in the room, it might be cozier to flank the hearth with a pair of smaller love seats or with a love seat facing the fire and two wing chairs set at right angles on either side—all taking advantage of a big coffee table or low bench.

If you must place the sofa against a wall, pull up a pair of club chairs (and ottomans) to create a companionable circle for family and friends. Try to keep some small chairs nearby so they can be pulled into the circle, when necessary, too.

Place the Largest Piece First

When planning any room arrangement, it is best to position the largest piece first and work out from there. In the living room, again, this piece might be the sofa or it might be a secretary, a full-wall entertainment system, an armoire holding the TV, or that TV itself if it is one of those huge projection TVs. Figure out how much room that big piece will take up and how other pieces of furniture must relate to it.

Will you have two massive pieces in the same room? If so, these should be placed so that they offset each other. If they are too close to each other, they will make that zone in the room seem crowded. They will make the room seem weighted in an awkward way. Usually, the best strategy for accommodating two large pieces is to place them opposite each other.

Move your templates around to see what arrangement will work best, and what will fit with room to spare.

Points to Consider

Designers concur on six points when they plan a furniture arrangement. These are as follows: focal point, balance, proportion, scale, harmony, and convenience.

The Focal Point

In order to feel immediately drawn into a room, it is important to establish a focal point. This is typically an architectural element, such as a fireplace, that captures your attention as soon as you enter the room. It may also be a fabulous view out a huge plate glass window. Or, if no specific point of interest exists, then the major piece of furniture may become the focal point. This is especially true of an entertainment center because its TV is an obvious attention-getter. In the master bedroom, the focal point is the bed.

Balance and Proportion

How the furnishings relate to each other is also important. Balance and proportion, therefore, are both critical to a sense of comfort and ease. If a spindly table is set down next to an overscaled chair, for instance, it can throw the entire furniture arrangement out of whack. Similarly, if an enormous dining table is surrounded by undersized chairs, then the entire suite—and room—will look strange.

Try to position individual pieces so that they look as if they belong together. Even if two nightstands do not match, for example, they will look better on either side of the bed if they are similar in size and if both are not dwarfed by the bed.

Scale

A sense of scale relates the furnishings, like people, to the overall space. The reason a ceiling is usually eight feet high is that adults range in height from approximately five to six feet, give or take a few inches. Furniture, too, looks best when it is not too tall or too short, relative to the height of the ceiling, nor too wide or too narrow, relative to the length and width of a room.

Designers are adept at playing with scale, and sometimes make quite a visual statement when they throw the scale off. If furnishings are kept to a minimum, for example, a designer might blow up the proportions of the sofa, say, or bring in a huge armoire that virtually touches the ceiling.

Playing with scale is tricky to pull off, though, unless you really know what you're doing. Instead, furnishings, both individually and as a suite, should feel right within the room, and that means their sizes should be consistent. This can be particularly important in a child's room; children, like Goldilocks, sense when their furniture is out of scale (especially when it is way too large) and they do not like it at all.

Harmony

Harmony is the overall impression given by the cohesive assembly of elements in a room. Harmony, in a way, consolidates the four preceding points. Without a focal point, balance, proportion, and scale, there would be no sense of harmony.

Convenience

And, finally, convenience counts. You want to be able to have the room work for you on every level and in every way. First of all, can everyone who comes into the room find a place to sit, be it on a sofa or chairs, or even on the floor? Do you have enough tabletops or other surfaces to put things on? Can you reach lamps easily when you want to turn them on or off?

Next, is the room easy to keep clean? Can you vacuum around the major pieces of furniture? Can you reach the windows, or are they blocked by something? Are surfaces too cluttered to dust?

Finally, can you move around the room with ease?

Traffic Patterns

When you devise your floor plan and furniture arrangement, you have to take into consideration how you move or travel through your room, from that room to another, and/or to the outdoors. You do not want to set up obstacles in your way.

Whether you are aware of it or not, you create invisible corridors through and across a room whenever you pass through it, even when you travel from one piece of furniture to another. This is what designers call a traffic pattern; every room has at least one, if not more.

Access and Egress

Certain traffic patterns through a room are dictated by the placement of the doors and windows. Access and egress should be easy; you do not want to block entry to or exit from a room, especially in an emergency. The swing of a door takes up about 36", in an arc. If you feel this arc will inhibit the way you want to furnish a room, you can change the orientation of the door by rehanging it so that it swings in the opposite direction, or so that it swings away from rather than into the room.

It is also a good idea to keep the area in front of the windows free of impediments so that you can open and close them or their window treatments without hassle.

Traffic and Furniture

How you use and arrange specific pieces of furniture will also affect how you move about a room. You want to be able to move in and around a group of furnishings without bumping into anything. You need clearance for this. For example, to be comfortable at a dinner table, you should allow at least 30″ to 36″ behind each chair so you can pull it out and away from the table. If the chair is occupied, you really should allow an additional foot so that someone can pass behind the occupant without feeling squeezed and so that the occupant doesn't feel pressured to move the chair in uncomfortably close to the table.

In the bedroom, you should leave plenty of clearance around the bed so that it can be made up easily. The size and width of the nightstands you select will probably dictate the width of the lanes on either side of the bed.

Traffic lanes in the bedroom also access closets and often a bathroom as well. Be sure you keep these lanes free of any obstruction, especially if you share your bedroom with another person.

Pulling Out Drawers

Consider, too, the placement of any chests of drawers. You will need to leave enough room to pull out drawers; you should allow about 30″ to 36″ for this. This goes for desk drawers and file drawers as well.

SOME COMMON CLEARANCES

Door swing	36″, in arc
Traffic lane	
through room	36″ wide
between pieces of furniture	24″–36″ wide
between sofa and coffee table	18″ wide
behind dining chairs and wall or sideboard	30″–36″ wide
around bed, to make it up	24″ on each side
Drawer pull-out	30″–36″ out

Once your furniture arrangements feel comfortable on your floor plan, you are ready to try them out at home. First, though, you want each room to be ready. It is easier to move furniture into and around a room in which the surfaces—ceiling, walls, and floor—are all set. In the next chapter we look at painting walls and ceilings, and, in the one that follows, you'll find out how to hang wall coverings. The chapter after that will discuss floors.

To Recap

- Play with furniture templates on your floor plan to figure out how your furniture can be comfortably arranged before making any new purchases.
- You can make your own miniature furniture pieces out of thick paper or cardboard. You may find collections of minis more flexible to work with, rather than tracing each template separately every time you alter your furniture arrangement.
- Consider cozy zones, or circles for seating, to foster conviviality in your living spaces.
- In any room, always establish a focal point first.
- Balance, proportion, and scale—how furnishings look and relate to each other—all contribute to how a room feels.
- Keep traffic lanes free so you can move easily around and through your rooms.
- Don't forget to plan for how far drawers pull out and how wide doors swing open.

PART TWO

Preparing the Background

CHAPTER 4

Painting Walls and Ceilings

Armed with floor plans, swatches, clippings, and notes, you are ready to start decorating. Before moving a single piece of furniture into your home (and before making any major purchases, if possible), it is a good idea to create a clean, crisp background for your things. The background is the canvas upon which you paint your personality; it comprises the walls and ceiling and floor of a room. First we will look at the ceiling and walls; later, the floor.

Perfectly Prepared Surfaces are Critical

Painting is easy; preparing walls and ceilings for painting is time-consuming and can be difficult. Paint will not adhere to a greasy, dirty, or blemished surface. Nor will the final results look good if the paint is slathered over a blistered, peeling, or pitted surface. Paint is cosmetic, but it will not camouflage surface ills. Indeed, a new coat of paint may only expose and reveal a poor surface. Therefore, it is essential that you or a professional of your choosing make all surfaces as smooth and blemish-free as possible.

An Empty Space

It is much easier to deal with surfaces if a room is empty. Furnishings not only take up a good deal of space, but massive pieces can be difficult to move about once set in place. If you have ever painted a completely furnished room, you no doubt recall the inconvenience of pushing everything into the center of the room, covering it all with drop cloths, and worrying about damage throughout the process, especially if the job took days to complete. So, try to paint before you furnish, if you can. If you cannot, of course, you will have to move furniture out of the room or cover it to protect it from drips.

A Landlord's Responsibility

If you are renting your place, your landlord usually assumes responsibility for the move-in condition of all of the surfaces, including a new coat of paint. Any surface repairs and painting should be completed before you move in. If your walls and ceiling do require repairs, check your lease to see what your landlord's obligation is to you. You may be able to negotiate to have expenses for repairs and subsequent painting deducted from your rent, either from the first month's or last month's rent, or from the security deposit. As a last recourse, you may be able to withhold rent until surfaces meet the specifications in the lease.

Read your lease thoroughly, too, before making any changes or improvements on your own. If you want to paint your rooms a color that is not the standard "landlord white," you may have to return the walls to the original state or pay a penalty. Talk to your landlord. He may okay your color choices and get the work done for you, or he may give you permission to paint your place yourself. If so, request his permission in writing and attach it to your lease to avoid arguments if or when you move out.

Evaluating Damage

When you purchase a house or apartment, chances are you will have to effect some repairs to any surfaces to be painted or papered unless it is a brand-new place.

The first thing to do is make a thorough inspection, both by eye and with a small pick and scraper. Are there blisters or bubbles that might indicate water damage behind old paint, paper, or plaster? If the ceilings and walls are plaster-coated, are there cracks? If so, how wide are these? Are they just feathery little localized hairline cracks, or do they appear to be deeper, jagged cracks that spread across a wide area? Does the ceiling or wall seem pitted in places? Are there any holes?

If ceilings and walls are constructed of drywall (also called Sheetrock), are they smooth? Do nailheads protrude? Has seam paper peeled back? Are there any pits or punctures?

Test blisters and cracks with a pick and/or scraper to check out the extent of any underlying damage.

Making Repairs Yourself

If the damage seems minor—just a few nicks or scratches or flaking places scattered over the surface—you can scrape or peel away the flakes or chips yourself or fill in nicks with Spackle, a gooey puttylike compound that looks like toothpaste.

Hairline cracks also can be repaired easily by laying a special paper tape, found at your home center, over the crack. The tape is bonded to the wall with a mixture called joint compound, which, though puttylike, too, is a bit thinner than Spackle.

When to Call in Professional Help

Sometimes when you pick away at a pit or crack in an old house with plaster walls, though, plaster falls away to reveal a serious problem. The cavity may turn out to be too big to fill with Spackle, or the wall may have to be resurfaced altogether.

If the damage turns out to be extensive, you may not want to make repairs yourself. Depending upon how handy you are, you may only require professional help for the application of new coats of plaster or for the installation of a new layer of drywall over the old plaster wall before you prime and paint (or paper) yourself. (Blueboard is the type of drywall that pros use to cover old plaster ceilings or walls; drywall is the generic name for the wallboard trademarked as Sheetrock. Both types come in sheets of various sizes and thicknesses; the $4' \times 8' \times \frac{1}{2}''$ size is the most common.)

Beware of Lead

Some repairs are prohibited by law. If surface cleanup involves extensive removal of lead-based paint, for instance, it should be done by a professional. Lead is poisonous. Federal laws regulating the removal and disposal of lead-based paint are complex. (All new paints are, by law, lead-free, but paints that are over twenty years old were not. No one knew for certain then that lead was hazardous to your health.)

One of the major hazards of paint removal is breathing in or ingesting lead particles. Sanding down old paint is extremely dangerous because the resulting paint dust fills the surrounding air. Using chemical solvents (many of which are toxic) to remove lead-infected paints is also hazardous. That is why it pays to hire a professional who is knowledgeable about the removal and disposal of hazardous materials.

If you decide to remove small amounts of lead-laden paint yourself, check local ordinances about how to pack up and contain the paint-infected debris. Check, too, on how to label the containers, and where they should be removed to. If you take them to a local dump, check to see where they must be deposited.

Safety First

Even if you are only going to remove a minimal amount of flakes and chips yourself, be sure you wear safety goggles to protect your eyes, a face filter mask or respirator that completely covers your nose and mouth, and rubber gloves to prevent cuts on your hands. These are all available in paint or hardware stores or home centers.

Be certain the room is adequately ventilated and that floors are completely covered with drop cloths so that they do not become impregnated with dust from paint and plaster or soiled by smeared paint. Drop cloths should be fastened with masking tape to the bottom of the baseboards so that they do not slip.

A last note of caution: Never smoke a cigarette or light a match in a room that contains chemicals that emit toxic fumes, such as paint removers, turpentine, or other inflammable or explosive products.

Washing Down Old Paint

Once small repairs are made and these areas are sanded and smoothed, the rest of the old paint often can be left alone. To prepare the surface, all you have to do is wash it down thoroughly with a liquid household cleanser or with a half-and-half solution of plain ammonia and water and then apply a coat of sizing, which is a gelatinlike liquid acrylic undercoat that feels slightly abrasive to the touch.

Removing Old Paint from Wood Trim

Paint removal is a tricky business because you have to use chemical solvents called paint removers or strippers. Many of these are flammable and emit highly toxic fumes, so look for the new generation of strippers that are less toxic to the environment and do not emit fumes. If the work is extensive, it may be best to leave this work to a professional, but if you have only an extremely limited area to strip such as the trim around a door, you **can** do this yourself—if you take the following precautions.

As mentioned above, *always* wear protective clothing. Cover your arms and legs completely because chemical solvents burn the skin. Wear industrial-weight rubber gloves to cover your hands. Safety goggles and a filter mask to cover your nose and mouth are mandatory gear for this work.

Limit the amount of time you work on stripping to about a half hour or so; take breaks and go outside for a breath of fresh air before returning to the project, if you can. You may feel lightheaded after awhile if you don't.

Always follow the manufacturer's instructions on the solvent's container explicitly—to the letter. Be sure the room is adequately ventilated to minimize fume buildup. Clean up and remove debris, as outlined above, in the safest way possible, in tightly covered, tightly wrapped containers. You must label these as hazardous waste for garbage pickup.

Once the old paint has been stripped off, go over the trim with a fine-grade steel wool to insure that it is completely smooth. Rub with a rag to remove any residue, and wash completely with a liquid household cleanser or with a half-and-half solution of ammonia and water.

Removing Old Wallpaper

Peeling off old wallpaper can reveal a plethora of injuries; in an old house, the wallpaper may be the only thing that is holding a plaster wall together. Indeed, in many older dwellings, many layers of wallpaper may have been applied, one right over the other.

Sometimes, if you are lucky, the vintage wallpaper may have dried out so much that it can simply be peeled off in strips. For papers that adhere, you will need to steam off the paper. You can rent a steamer from your local home center. If you cannot find a steamer, you can work with sponges and water, but this takes more time. The steam or water saturates the paper and softens the glue bonding the paper to the wall. Once the paper and glue are softened, they can be scraped off with a wide putty knife.

If the wallpaper is covering drywall, which is usually the case in recently built houses or apartments, you should take care not to oversaturate the paper. You do not want to remove the protective paper covering the drywall when you remove the wallpaper.

Paste residue can be washed off with a solution of white vinegar and water, mixed in a ratio of one to four.

Removing Vinyl Wall Coverings

There are several types of vinyl wall covering. The easiest to remove is strippable wall covering, which is backed with fabric. This type peels off the wall, leaving only a paste residue. Paper-backed vinyl can be peeled off in strips, too, but it leaves its backing on the wall. Once the outer layer has been removed, the backing must be soaked and scraped off with a wide putty knife, as you would remove wallpaper. If you did not install the wall covering you are peeling off, you may not be able to identify which kind it is until you start to peel off the first strip.

Vinyl-coated wall covering, which tends to be thicker than the strippable types, cannot be stripped or peeled off in one go. Instead, it first must be punctured with holes and drenched with water. The water penetrates to, and saturates the backing so that the wall covering can be scraped off the wall.

In all cases, any paste that remains on the wall must be washed off with a vinegar/water solution and the wall must be repaired, if necessary, and sanded smooth before painting.

When to Leave Wallpaper Alone

If old wallpaper is in good repair and its seams lie flat, you may want to leave it alone, and not bother with the hassle of removing it. If you are going to paint the room, you can do so right over the old paper, if you like. Because wallpaper is porous, it will suck up some paint, but a second coat will seal the surface.

Plastering

When repairs are complete, the walls can be made ready for paint. If your walls are plaster and need to be completely replastered, it is best to call in a pro. Plaster is not easy to work with, and two or three coats are necessary to create a smooth surface. Also, plaster raises a huge amount of dust, so the room being plastered has to be closed off completely, or the dust will seep into every nook and cranny in your whole place.

Final Preparations

Once the walls, ceilings, and trim are repaired and smoothed, you are almost ready to paint. It is a good idea to mask all electrical outlets and switch plates to protect them from paint drips; simply cover them with masking tape. You can remove them, which allows you to paint all the way up to the openings, but wires will be exposed; in this case, you should turn off all electricity to the room to avoid the hazard of electrocution.

Lay drop cloths over the entire floor, making sure that they hug the baseboards so that no errant drip can seep behind and under the drop cloth onto the floor.

If you do not want to remove ceiling fixtures, wrap them in plastic. If you have track lighting, apply masking tape to the edges so that you won't get paint on the track. Remove the individual fixtures from the track or tape plastic bags over them.

Types of Paint

Most interior painting today is done with water-soluble, easy-to-clean-up-after latex paints. For the do-it-yourselfer, these are the easiest to work with, and the newest paints emit little or no odor, either, so the actual task of painting is pleasant. Latex paints have been improved over the years in terms of durability and they dry quickly; in fact, you can apply a second coat almost immediately after the first.

Designers often recommend oil-based paints for areas such as kitchens and baths that are vulnerable to moisture and grease because they feel they are easier to clean. They also prefer oil-based paints for wood paneling and trim. Oil-based paints are messy to work with, though, especially if they require thinners such as turpentine to facilitate application. Oil-based paints are smelly, and they take a long time to dry; you must leave the surface alone for at least twenty-four hours between coats. Pale colors, especially white, tend to yellow over time. For all these reasons, most do-it-yourselfers should stick with latex paints, even for walls that need to be washed often.

Some Special Considerations

Latex paints will not adhere to oil-based paints and vice versa. A light sanding and/or sizing and a primer coat are essential to ensure that the final coat adheres and maintains a smooth texture.

The primer coat is usually simply a base coat of white that masks the old surface wall and covers any spots that might exist if the wall has not been resurfaced with plaster or drywall. Because the primer coat is hidden, it can be, and usually is, a less expensive paint (and white is less expensive to buy than a color, which must be mixed).

Working with Colors

When working with colors, it is a good idea to try out or experiment with small amounts on the wall before buying the quantity you will finally need. Certain colors jump at you; others seem to recede. Bright colors energize and grayed-out colors soothe. A dark color will visually lower a ceiling; dark walls tend to close a room in, especially if the ceiling is also dark. Pale walls, conversely, can make a small room appear larger.

If you are combining colors, play them off against each other to see if one affects your perception of the other. Some colors make their companions appear stronger than they really are; others can stifle or mute adjacent hues.

Paint chips tend to give the impression of a paler hue; in other words, the actual paint—once painted on the wall—often appears darker than on the chip. That is why it is best to experiment with doses of real paint and not just trust a chip. Paint stores will let you purchase as little as a pint of a ready-mixed color. If you want a custom hue, the minimum purchase is one quart. Brush swatches on your walls and check how the colors look both in daylight and under lamplight. You may have to try out several hues before you make your final decision.

Considering Finishes

Paint, whatever the hue, comes in a variety of finishes. The finish most commonly desired for walls and ceilings is a flat finish that displays a matte or nonshiny appearance. A flat finish also slightly mutes or masks the intensity of a color.

A satin or eggshell finish has a slight sheen and is often used for trim and other wood surfaces including doors. A satin finish may also be used for a bathroom or kitchen because it wipes down more easily than a flat finish. It is also often smart to use in children's rooms for the same reason.

Semigloss paints are slightly shinier; high-gloss paints are extremely shiny and are usually used for special effects. Some people like a high-gloss look for a bathroom, for instance, because it is reflective and makes the room seem larger. Some people like to contrast flat walls with high-gloss trim for visual interest.

How Paint Is Sold

Paint comes in pints, quarts, and gallons. Paint for a room is usually calculated on a per-gallon basis. A gallon of primer, the underlying base coat that is used to cloak the plaster or drywall, normally covers about 180 square feet of wall surface. (See section below to translate this amount to your needs.) A gallon of latex paint should cover about 270 square feet of wall surface, depending upon the quality of the paint.

Paints vary a great deal. Best-quality paints are thick, smooth, and creamy, spread easily, and cover surfaces well in one or two coats over a primer coat. Inferior paints tend to be thin and runny. With a thin paint you have to go over the same area again and again to build up a surface free of roller or brush marks; in this case, you will need more paint and so savings are negligible.

In fact, as with anything you purchase, it is recommended that you buy the best you can afford. You will save money in the long run because better-quality products last longer, too.

Calculating Your Wall Space and Your Exact Paint Needs

To calculate how much paint you will need to cover the walls of a room, multiply the perimeter of the room by the height of the room from the ceiling to the baseboard, in inches. Divide by twelve to arrive at the square footage, and round up. Divide again, by three, to arrive at the square yardage.

Some paint stores advise you to subtract the surface taken up by windows and doors; it is better that you **not** do this. It is a good idea, instead, to keep extra paint on hand for touch-ups later on, especially if you special-order a color. Indeed, it can be difficult—if not impossible—to match a color with precision once paint has been ordered and the job is completed. Because colors are made by mixing incremental amounts of concentrated tints to white, paint color can—and often does—vary from batch to batch, even when mixed the same day. Order more than you think you will need.

Paint for the Ceilings

You should decide on the paint for your ceiling at the same time. The easiest solution is to paint all of your ceilings a flat white. Once again, calculate the square yardage of each ceiling, then add up the figures to arrive at the total for all your ceilings.

Painting Trim and Doors

It is recommended that you paint your trim and doors *before* painting the walls, but after the ceiling. Once the trim has been given both its base and its top coats, and has dried, you should tape it off with masking tape so that the wall paint does not drool onto your just-completed work. (If you think you will create drips when you paint your walls, leave the baseboards and paint them last, after the walls.)

Depending upon how much woodwork is in the room, you should be able to get away with a single gallon of paint for this job. If you decide to use an oil-based paint, you should know that it covers about ten fewer square yards than a latex paint.

Tools of the Trade

After selecting your paint, you must assemble the rest of your tools. For optimum coverage, it is recommended that you purchase high-quality rollers and brushes. For walls, you will probably want to use a 9″ roller to cover the main areas; it takes much less time to roll a wall than to brush it, even though you will have to use a brush to reach into corners and edges where a roller will not fit.

Rollers and Roller Covers

You should select a napped roller cover made of a synthetic fiber, usually Orlon or a Dynel blend, for flat latex paints. Nap feels wooly and comes in three thicknesses. The ⅜″-thick nap is preferred for walls that are completely smooth; its wool is denser and leaves no traces of texture. For textured or rough walls, such as those that emulate coarsely trowled stucco, you can choose between a ½″ or a ¾″ thick nap; these will reach into the little indentations created by the rugged texture. For semigloss paints, use a mohair roller cover with a ¼″-thick nap. In every case, the nap should feel soft all over and be free of lumps or loose fibers that could mat or become gluey when saturated with paint.

The roller cover slides onto a metal roller and should fit snugly so it will not slide around when in use. The metal roller should be securely attached to its handle so that the roller and its cover will rotate together smoothly, without jerking. The handle should feel comfortable in your hand. If you are painting a ceiling or a very high wall, you can add an extender to the handle.

If you want to roll most of your trim, a 2″-wide roller works best. Most pros prefer brushes for trim and for doors because brushes are easier to control. (Rollers and brushes used for oil-based paints should be made of natural materials, rather than synthetics. Real wool or hog's hair are the materials most often recommended.)

Best Brushes

The brushes you will need to cut into the edges of both the walls and the trim should measure 2″ in width. The best brushes for latex paints are made with nylon bristles or bristles in a Dynel blend. The bristles should feel smooth yet firm when you press them in any direction. They should also taper to a chisellike edge. When you spread the bristles apart, you will see a center plug (where the handle attaches), but the plug should not create a big hollow where paint could collect and cause erratic dripping or dribbling.

You may want to keep a 4"-wide brush on hand, too, for wider applications. It is always a good idea to have several brushes at the ready so that you can switch off as you move from ceiling to trim to wall.

You will also need paint trays (one for each color or finish); assorted rags—both damp and dry—to clean brushes and spills; and cans (old coffee cans work well) for same; masking tape to mask off edges; drop cloths and/or newspapers, and a sturdy stepladder to get to hard-to-reach spots and ceilings. If you work with oil-based paints, you will need turpentine and paint thinner, too, both to thin thickened paint and to clean brushes.

Loading the Paint

When you work with a roller, soak the roller cover evenly all around to insure a smooth roll-out. Roll off excess paint onto the ribbed portion of the paint tray. If there are any drips on the handle of the roller, wipe them off with a rag.

When you work with a brush, dip the bristles only one-third of the way into the paint so that paint won't leak down into the hollow at the handle end. Rub off excess, from one side of the brush only, on the edge of the paint can or paint tray.

Start with the Ceiling

It may sound obvious, but you should always start with the ceiling. Be sure the ceiling is completely clean and free of dust or grease before applying any paint, to avoid streaking.

Although it may seem easier to stand on the floor and apply ceiling paint with a long-handled roller, you might find you have more control if you work with a short roller or with a wide brush from atop a stepladder. Paint trays come with grips that attach directly to the ladder so that you will not need to come down off the ladder except to refill the tray.

Brush on a Band First

For the best job, first brush on a 2"-wide band around the perimeter of the ceiling, at its junction with the walls or cornice molding. You don't have to measure the band; a 2"-wide brush sets the guide. After painting on the band, gently feather the edge facing into the ceiling to eliminate any lip or seam; feathering just means that you blur the edges of the band by dragging a dry brush across and over the edge.

Roll out from the band toward the center of the ceiling in small, manageable sections. The easiest amount of surface to cover at one go measures about four feet square. As you roll on the paint, overlap the band as much as possible to ensure a smooth, seamless transition and to camouflage the fact that the band is there.

After rolling over a section in one direction, turn the roller ninety degrees and reroll over the same area. Turn the roller back again, and reroll a third time. Three passes should ensure that the coat is free of roller marks. Make sure, as you move from section to section, to feather their seams so that all the sections will blend together.

A Second Coat?

If you have rolled each section of the ceiling three times, as outlined above, you may not need to apply a second coat. Wait until the ceiling is completely dry and inspect it closely to see if any seams show or if the paint is at all uneven.

If so, apply a second coat in the same manner as the first.

Beginning the Walls

Before tackling the wide-open surfaces of your walls, brush a frame of bands around the perimeter of each wall, just as you did on the ceiling. Work your way across the top, just below the ceiling line, then move down the walls at the corners, and finally run a band along the baseboard or at the junction with the floor. Feather the inside edge, as you did on the ceiling, to avoid leaving a lip of paint that could form a line when it dries.

Always paint walls from top to bottom. Gravity pulls paint and you can smooth over any drips as you proceed downward.

The first layer of paint, or primer, is often tinted a pale shade of the final coat. Most professionals apply two coats over the primer to attain the smoothest surface possible.

Rolling Ms and Ws

Many professionals also counsel painting swaths of paint onto the wall in the following manner: Begin in one corner of the room and roll across and down, working on one 4'-square area at a time. Starting at a point about halfway down the wall, roll a large M or a W up to and over the band running along the ceiling line. Then, turn the roller ninety degrees and roll paint in horizontal bands across the letter to smooth out and fill in the spaces. Finally, return the roller to the vertical, and roll over the area a third time. If you keep your movements relaxed and steady, the procedure should go fairly quickly. As with the ceiling, roll onto all the bands as far as possible and always feather the seams between painted areas to eliminate a lip.

Painted Effects

You may find it fun to reproduce a painted effect on your wall. Painted effects add a sense of depth and texture. Of all painted effects, sponging, stippling, and combing are the easiest to execute. Other effects include stenciling, marbleizing, and woodgraining. These require a little more expertise, but if you have the time and inclination, all are fun to try. Kits for the latter are available at craft shops; always follow manufacturer's instructions.

Materials You'll Need for Basic Effects

All you need to sponge are, obviously, sponges—preferably big, lightweight, natural ones, which are available at better drugstores. These can be quite costly, however. If you find them too expensive, look for synthetic sponges that are as porous and flexible as possible. For stippling, you only need a couple of artist's paintbrushes of various thicknesses, but all should taper to a point. Art supply or craft shops carry rubber combs for combing, or you can make your own comb from heavy cardboard. Cut a rectangle from the cardboard in a size that you can hold easily, and then just cut notches or teeth along one edge, about two inches deep, in the thickness or thicknesses you desire.

For all three effects, the underlying base coat should be a semigloss or a high-gloss finish, not a flat finish. The finished effect

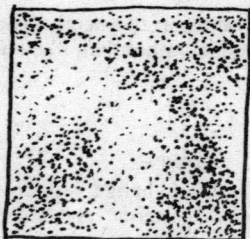

Stipple Effect

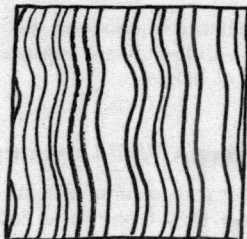

Combing Effect

looks better and flat paint will inhibit the movement of a comb, too.

Sponge Painting

To sponge, simply dab the sponge into the paint. Pat any excess off on a piece of newspaper or a paper towel until the sponge is almost dry. Then dab at random over the surface of the wall, overlapping edges as you go until you build up the texture to the consistency or look that appeals to you. The sponging can be very airy or it can appear very dense. It is up to you to decide.

Stippling

To stipple, dip the paintbrush into the paint and gently blot any excess off onto a newspaper or paper towel. Then apply stipples— or dots—in a random fashion over the surface of the wall. The overall effect will appear somewhat granular; again, you can try for a look that is airy or dense. You can alter the look, too, by using different size brushes, which will vary the size of the dots.

Comb Painting

To comb, dip the teeth of your comb into the paint and wipe the excess off one side against your paint can or tray. Drag the comb over the surface of the wall, from top to bottom. Try to run the comb as far down the wall as possible. If you cannot travel down the full length, overlap the tail of the first pull just slightly. You may have to feather the individual lines with a narrow artist's brush to blend them.

As you move from one side of the wall to the other, try to match the combed bands as closely as you can. Do not overlap them, though. Leave a slight gap between them. This gap looks best when it equals one that exists between two teeth. The final effect will look like a continuous pattern, rather than like a jarring series of bands.

Hanging a Wall Covering

A faster way to achieve texture on a wall is to hang a wall covering, because they come in so many styles, patterns, and colors that choosing one will prove an extremely effective way to give your walls a distinct personality. A wall covering can also match or coordinate with a fabric; in fact, many fabric manufacturers have added wall coverings to their collections for this purpose. Hanging a wall covering is not difficult, either. However, many landlords will not allow wall coverings, so if you are renting your place, check your lease to see if you can install a wall covering and obtain written permission before you do any work.

To Recap

- Painting is easy. Preparing surfaces—ceilings and walls—takes more time.
- Surfaces should be smooth and free of blemishes so that your final coat of paint will be smooth, look good, and adhere properly.
- Care must be taken when removing old paint, especially lead-based paint, which is poisonous.
- A paint job looks best when finest-quality paints and brushes and/or rollers are used.
- Latex paint is easiest to work with.
- Choose a paint finish for the specific effect you want. Most walls look best with a flat finish and trim with an eggshell or semigloss finish. A high-gloss finish is usually used to create a glowing, reflective surface.
- If you feel like it, why not try out a painted effect, such as sponging, stippling, or combing?
- Try hanging a wall covering to achieve texture on your walls.

CHAPTER 5

Fixing Up Your Floors

Unless you are building a house from scratch or plan to undertake a major remodeling, you will move into a house or apartment where the floors are a given. In other words, the decision regarding the type of permanent flooring laid down in the various rooms in your new home will already have been made by the home builder or by the landlord.

Changing the flooring is a costly process. Old flooring, though, usually can be covered over or—if it is wood—it can be refinished.

A Brief History

Before World War II, the floors in houses were made of wood because trees were plentiful. In the postwar boom, especially in the burgeoning suburbs, and with the advent of new building technologies, traditional plank or strip-style hardwood flooring began to be supplanted by a plywood base covered with wall-to-wall carpeting or, in some areas, with parquet squares. Synthetic flooring made of asbestos or vinyl proved the most popular and economical choice for the kitchen, and for many baths, too, because synthetics resist moisture.

Softwood versus Hardwood

Settlers in the original thirteen colonies made do with the wood at hand, typically pine, which is a softwood. (Softwoods, such as pine, come from evergreen trees that bear cones and needles; hardwoods, such as oak and maple, from leafy, deciduous trees.) In those days, wide planks could be sawn and milled from logs of robust dimensions. Some early or historic houses exhibit planks that measure eighteen inches to two feet across. Planks today rarely exceed one foot in width because logs are milled when trees are younger.

The disadvantage of softwood is that it pits and scars easily; it is, indeed, soft. Many traditionalists, though, like the look of wide-plank flooring. For this reason, some manufacturers make hardwood flooring that emulates the softwood planks used by our ancestors. The new planks are actually a great deal narrower, though—no more than six inches wide. Some of these versions come complete with darker circular plug inserts that mimic the old-time pegs that held the planks in place.

Hardwood Flooring

If you inherit hardwood flooring throughout your new home, consider yourself lucky. Hardwood flooring—usually oak, but sometimes lighter-colored maple or ash—is extremely durable, and, if not severely damaged, it can be refinished to suit your taste without breaking your budget.

Hardwood floors often were stained dark and then waxed or polished and buffed to a fine sheen to showcase formal furnishings; in recent years, as Americans have leaned toward a more relaxed and eclectic decorating style, the trend in many parts of the country has turned away from shiny dark floors toward a lighter look. Old floors, therefore, are often sanded to reveal their natural, lighter cast. Once sanded, they may be stained again, but in a lighter

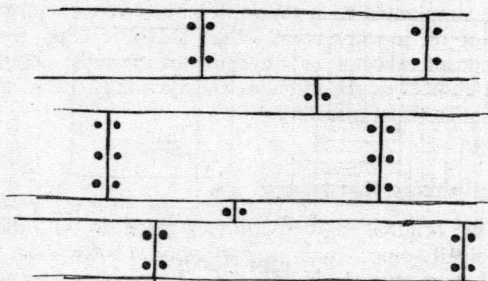

Random Width Planks with Pegs

tone, then sealed or waxed or brushed with a moisture-resistant polyurethane or waterborne protective coating in a satin or matte finish.

Hardwood Strips

Hardwood flooring is typically laid out in narrow, parallel strips, in an all-over linear pattern that presents a uniform look. Sometimes the floor is accentuated by a border created by inserting narrow strips of wood stained a darker hue.

Random-strip flooring comprises strips of varying widths that alternate in two or three widths across the surface of the floor. Random-strip floors give a more casual appearance.

Today, strip flooring has been precut, prefinished, and prepackaged in cartons to make it easy for the do-it-yourselfer to purchase flooring, take it home, and install it.

Other Hardwood Patterns

The days of 18"-wide floorboards are long past, but plank flooring—with or without mock pegs—remains a popular choice. Today's planks typically measure 48" in length; widths vary from 2" to 6". You may want all your planks to be of similar width, or you may prefer a random-width appearance.

Parquet, often found in postwar dwellings, consists of small strips laid out in patterns that are contained in and defined as squares. The most familiar parquet pattern is the basket weave.

Today, parquet flooring comes preassembled in blocks, like tiles. Blocks usually measure 9" square. Only in the most expensive custom installations is parquet still laid down piece by piece.

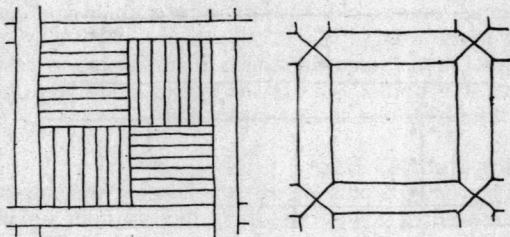

Parquet Floors

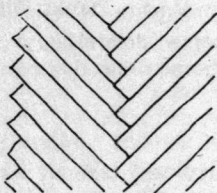

Herringbone

Herringbone is also a familiar alternative. Herringbone strips are narrow and short and lock together in a V-formation familiar from the tweed of the same name.

A single carton of flooring covers between 9 and 20 square feet, depending upon the product; read the label on the carton to find out how many square feet your preferred product—be it strip or parquet—will cover.

Do-It-Yourself Flooring

Strips, planks, and parquet blocks are fairly easy for the handy do-it-yourselfer to lay down. Strips and planks have been designed so that they will fit and lock together, protruding tongue into inset groove. Parquet blocks fit snugly, abutting edge to edge.

Calculate the square footage of your floor and divide by the square footage indicated on the box of parquet of your choice. The figure you arrive at will tell you how many cartons will be necessary for the job. It is wise to buy an extra carton because some parquet squares will have to be cut to fit around baseboards and jogs in the wall.

A special note: Some flooring is foam-backed to cushion the impact of foot traffic. Ask for the proper adhesive to bond this type of flooring to the surface underneath.

Preparing the Old Floor

First, of course, you must prepare the flooring underneath. Flooring manufacturers counsel checking the old floor for moisture. Does the floor—be it concrete, plywood, or old wood—feel damp? If so, you should have your house or apartment checked for leaks and get them repaired before attempting to lay down a new floor. Is old wood warped or buckled? New wood will also warp and buckle if laid down on a damp floor.

The old floor, be it concrete, plywood, or old flooring, must be absolutely clean and smooth and free of pits or blemishes. Patch it, if necessary; nail holes and cracks in wood can be filled with a putty specified for this purpose. If the floor is uneven, it may have to be sanded, too.

Sanding, as you will learn later in this chapter, is an arduous task and probably should be done by a professional.

Laying the Flooring

Besides the flooring adhesive and a spreading tool recommended by the manufacturer or floor supply company, a rubber-headed mallet is the only tool you need. Basically, all you have to do is glue down the strips or planks, then hammer them together to ensure a tight fit. Parquet blocks are glued, too, then pounded flat. Always follow the manufacturer's instructions to the letter, though. Products do vary.

Preserving Existing Wood Floors

Getting your floors in shape can be one of the best decisions—and investments—you can make in your home. Well-finished floors will last for years. If you can, refinish your floors **before** you paint or apply wall covering to your walls—and preferably before you move in.

Over time, wood flooring can discolor and become worn in areas that are highly trafficked. Usually, though, a wood floor can be brought back to its original luster in a three-part refinishing process.

The first, or preparatory stage, involves sanding and scraping away old wax, soil, and paint, if any. Next comes an application of color, be it a dark wood tone, a pale pastel, or whitewashlike stain. Lastly, the floor is sealed and/or protected with polyurethane or with a waterborne finish or with paste wax. If your rooms are small, you can easily tackle at least the final two stages of this kind of job. Huge floors, though, probably should be handled by a pro.

Sanding the Floors
Before you refinish a wood floor, you most likely will have to sand and scrape it. This is a difficult and heavy job and one that is extremely dusty and noisy. For this reason, flooring supply companies recommend that sanding be done by a professional.

Renting Sanders
If you feel you can tackle the job, though, floor sanders can be rented from a large hardware store or from outlets listed under "Floor Machines—Renting" in your Yellow Pages. There are two types of sanders. The drum sander operates by rotating a horizontal drum that is covered by the sandpaper. A disc sander rotates a disc of sandpaper. Some are dustless, with a detachable bag that should collect up to 90 percent of the sawdust.

Heavy and Hard to Manage
A floor sander is a heavy piece of equipment (they weigh ninety pounds or more), that can gouge your floor if mishandled. Ask for a demonstration before you take the sander home. You will learn that you must keep the machine moving in a slow, continuous, even, and level motion, and you must stop and start the machine with the drum or disc placed firmly on the floor. If you tilt the machine, you will gouge the wood.

Because sanders raise an immense amount of dust and are extremely noisy, too, wear protective gear, including goggles, a respirator mask, and ear protectors.

Before You Begin
Before sanding, hammer in any protruding nails below the surface of the wood so they will not catch on and tear the sandpaper. Vacuum up any accumulated soils and dust.

A Three-Pass Process

Sanding requires at least three passes with sandpapers of varying grits from coarse to fine. If you are sanding strips or planks, be sure the sander travels with the grain of the wood on every pass. If you are smoothing parquet, travel in an X across the room from corner to corner, and then make a third pass parallel to the length of the room.

Finishing the Job

To complete a sanding job, you will have to rent an edger, too. An edger is a small, hand-held sander that can be manipulated into hard-to-reach spots such as corners, as well as hug baseboards.

After sanding, use a scraper to pry up any resistant splinters or chips.

Wood Stains

Raw wood is surprisingly light in color. To achieve the colors or tones that we readily associate with certain woods, stain must be applied.

Stains are known by the woods they evoke: mahogany, cherry, walnut, ebony, teak. To this list can be added the pale stains equated with pickling or bleaching: wheat, gray, and white. (Bleaching is caustic and is usually done by a professional; the pale stains that you can apply look just as fine.)

Check out the variety of toner/stains offered by the floor supplies outlet; some are quick-drying. Others, usually with built-in sealers, take longer to dry.

Applying Stains

Stains, both light and dark, penetrate the wood. All you need are clean, dry rags to wipe the stain on and into the wood. Keep wiping until you achieve the depth of tone you desire.

Pickling is, in a way, a form of whitewashing; you wipe the pale stain into the wood in the same manner as you would a dark tone. Whitewashing is done with paint, but the application is similar. Brush on a thin coat of paint; then, with rags, rub the paint into the wood until it looks the way you want it to.

In all of the above processes, work in one small area at a time and rub seams together to avoid streaking.

Waxing and Lacquering

Wood gently expands and contracts with heat and cold. Traditionally, wood floors were waxed and polished to a high gloss. Waxing is still highly recommended, because paste wax allows the floorboards to breathe. Waxing, though, requires continual upkeep. To maintain their sheen, floors should be buffed often (as often as twice a week in trafficked areas), and rewaxed periodically. Old wax should be removed from time to time, too, as soil becomes embedded in it, discoloring the wood.

Lacquer is another finish that was traditionally applied. Lacquers, however, are extremely flammable, so most floor supply companies will not work with them.

Protecting with Polyurethane

An alternative to lacquer is oil-modified polyurethane, which provides a virtually maintenance-free finish. Polyurethaned floors need only be swept and/or damp mopped. Over time, polyurethane yellows, however, so it can affect the appearance of a light-hued floor.

Applying polyurethane is a bit risky for the novice. Polyurethane is smelly, releases toxic fumes, and is combustible, so you must rent or buy goggles, gloves, and a respirator mask to protect your eyes, nose, skin, and hands. You must ventilate the room and you cannot smoke or light a match nearby for at least twenty-four hours.

Brush on the finish much as you would a coat of paint, following the grain of the wood. Allow the coat of polyurethane to dry thoroughly (at least twenty-four hours). Gently sand by hand with a fine-grit sandpaper, using a circular motion, before applying the next coat. You will need three coats to attain a good finish.

Polyurethane comes in four lusters: matte, satin, semigloss, and gloss. Most floors look best with a satin finish, because it looks neither too flat not too shiny, but some people prefer a much glossier look. It's really just a matter of taste which finish you select. Ask to see samples at your flooring supplies company if you cannot decide which is best for you.

A final point to remember: Floor finishes dry best when they are applied on a warm, relatively dry day. (The optimum is seventy degrees and 50 percent humidity.)

Waterborne Protectors

The newest generation of finishes are odor-free, fast-drying waterborne finishes, which are not dangerous to work with. They are easy to brush on and easy to maintain. They also do not yellow. They do not resist moisture, though, quite as well as polyurethane; oil, which is present in polyurethane, repels water better. Two applications add up to a good-looking surface; allow it to dry thoroughly, as you would if you applied polyurethane, and sand lightly between coats.

Painting a Wood Floor

After sanding your floor, you may decide to paint it instead of staining it or whitewashing it.

The paint you select for a floor should be chip-proof. One durable type is marine deck paint. This type of paint was originally developed for boats which, obviously, must withstand the vagaries of weather. Deck paints, like paints actually specified for porches and for concrete floors, are ideal candidates for rooms that will receive a great deal of traffic, such as a kitchen, child's room, potting shed, mudroom, or laundry, and, of course, an indoor or outdoor porch. All of the above paints are offered in a fairly narrow range of colors.

A Narrow Palette

A painted floor makes a statement. Because a floor is such a broad surface, it's best to play it safe in terms of a choice of hue. Most floor paint colors fall within a fairly narrow range of colors, and many of them would be considered neutrals: linen, taupe, sage green, pale gray, or charcoal. To this list, add forest green, barn red, mustard, smoky blue, and dark blue.

Once the floor is sanded smooth and primed, roll or brush on two or three layers of paint, sanding between each, to build up a smooth, consistent surface. Don't forget to allow the paint to dry twenty-four hours before applying the next coat.

Painted Patterns

You can leave the floor plain or embellish it with stencils, stipples (random dots), or another faux finish, such as combing, which consists of random-width straight or wiggly lines that emulate the impressions created by a wide-tooth comb. All of these finishes are very easy to execute. If you don't want everyone's shoes to scuff your handiwork, you should seal it with polyurethane or a waterborne finish afterward.

FAUX FINISHES

Spattering   Dip end of bristle brush in paint; flick brush over floor surface. Spatters or drops will land at random. Keep flicking, with one color or more, until you achieve the texture or buildup of colored dots that you like.

Stippling   This is basically the same process, but you dip the end of a pointed artist's brush in the paint and directly apply dots to the floor. You can control the texture better by stippling. Stippling obviously takes longer, though.

Sponging   Dip a natural or synthetic sponge in paint; tap on paper until almost dry. (Natural sponges give a blurrier effect than synthetic ones.) Daub over floor in a random pattern. Build up pattern until you achieve the density you prefer. Synthetic sponges can also be used as is or cut into a shape to create or simulate a specific look, such as a herringbone brick pattern.

Combing   You can buy combs for painting at art supply stores, or you can make your own. Cut teeth into one side of a piece of thick poster board or cardboard. Brush or roll a coat of paint over your floor's base coat. While the paint is still wet, drag the comb through the paint, cleaning residue off the teeth often as you go. You can manipulate the comb to create wiggly lines, if you like.

Stenciling   Stencil kits are available at craft shops and art supply stores. Decide on whether you want to stencil over the entire floor or just create a border. It is best to mark where stencils will go beforehand. Lay the stencil in place and secure it with masking tape. Dip the stencil brush into paint and then blot on paper until almost dry. Dab over stencil (this is called *pouncing*), working from the center to the edges of the stencil in a circular motion. Keep pouncing until you achieve the density you like. Remove stencil and move it to the next position. Continue until pattern is completed. If you are just creating a border, simply travel in a line, or band, around the edges of the room, stencil by stencil.

Ceramic Tile

Ceramic tile is utilized in a variety of ways throughout the house, from backsplashes (the band of tile that protects the wall behind the stove and sink) and countertops in the kitchen to shower enclosures in the bath.

Ceramic tile used for flooring is heavier and more durable than that used on walls or other surfaces because it must withstand the impact of traffic and the weight of furnishings.

If you inherit ceramic tile in your new home, you may simply opt to retain what you have because pulling out a ceramic floor and replacing it with a like material or with another flooring is extremely costly. You can clean out and replace faulty or discolored grout and buff up the old tile to a new luster if the tiles are in good condition. Some sprinkling of hairline cracks across the surface of the tiles will not break through the glaze and should not be a problem, even in a shower stall.

Tile Applications

Because ceramic tile is usually glazed to a matte, satin, or gloss finish, it is impervious to moisture and, therefore, a logical choice for the kitchen, bath, entry, mudroom, and the vestibule just inside an entry. On the other hand, because ceramic tile is so hard, it is not a good choice for bedrooms or children's rooms.

Ceramic Mosaics

Ceramic tile comes in several sizes and myriad shapes. The smallest of these are mosaics. Mosaics are usually square, but are occasionally round. They are typically preset in sheets on a webbed backing so that they can be installed quickly, sheet by sheet. Mosaics look especially appealing in bathrooms or small entryways.

When you order mosaics, you can ask for sheets of mosaic in the same color, or you can request that a pattern be custom designed and assembled for your particular situation. Some popular mosaic patterns replicate American quilt designs; others mimic checkerboards. A field of plain mosaics may be outlined with a custom-designed tile border.

Ceramic Squares

Most ceramic tile is offered in squares, which range from the mosaic (which is a 1″ square) to a 12″ or 13″ square. Large squares give an impression of amplified space, especially when set on the bias, or diagonal. In kitchens and baths, large squares are often teamed with smaller squares on the walls. The squares most commonly requested for flooring applications are the 2″ in bathrooms and the 8″ in kitchens. The 4″ and 6″ sizes are more often reserved for walls, backsplashes, and countertops.

The color palette is wide and varied, and a vast assortment of patterns are available, such as those emulating traditional European or Middle Eastern motifs. Pictorial tiles are also available. Some scenic designs and still lifes are created from several tiles configured to form a big mural.

Terra-cotta Tile

One of the favored tiles for kitchens is made from terra-cotta, a mellow, rosy clay. Most terra-cotta tiles imported to this country come from Mexico. These are unglazed and so are very porous. They should be sealed with polyurethane to counteract grease and moisture.

Terra-cotta tiles come in squares and also in other shapes such as rectangles, hexagons, and octagons, which are often installed with small infill squares inset at the corners.

A more durable type of clay tile is the quarry tile, which is extremely hard, with a crystalline surface. Quarry tiles are used for high-traffic areas, especially in commercial installations. Colors range from deep brown to a mustardy hue.

Terra-cotta tiles and quarry tiles, like ceramic tiles, are difficult to install, especially if they have to be cut to fit around cabinetry or built-in furnishings. Tile, in other words, should be installed by a professional.

Sheet Vinyl

The successor to linoleum, sheet vinyl flooring is the most popular choice for kitchens and baths in most new home construction. For the remodeler, sheet vinyl pays off, too, because a new layer can be laid right over the old one with little hassle. Sheet vinyl should be installed by a professional because of its weight and bulk and because it requires tailored cutting to fit around cabinetry or other obstacles.

Sheet vinyls, for the most part, replicate their more costly counterparts, wood and ceramic tile. Like carpet, vinyl is often displayed at your home center or kitchen design outlet in a waterfall, a big book of samples standing on a pedestal; you flip back the samples, like pages, to see them. You can ask for a small sample to take home.

Sheet vinyl is extremely easy to maintain, requiring only a light sponging to remove most spills.

Vinyl Tile

An alternative for the do-it-yourselfer is vinyl tile, which is the successor to asbestos tile, since asbestos is no longer legal. Vinyl tiles usually are less expensive per square foot than sheet vinyl. Some commercial-grade tiles (those used primarily in hospitals, schools, and offices) are coming onto the consumer market, too; these tend to cost more because they are thicker than vinyl tiles made for houses.

With adhesives recommended by the manufacturer and a special sawtooth-edged trowel, vinyl tiles are relatively easy to lay down. They can be installed over old linoleum or vinyl flooring, over a good plywood subfloor, or even over old hardwood if it is smooth and free of bumps.

Buying Vinyl Tile

Most vinyl tile comes in 12″ squares. Divide the length of the room by twelve. How many squares does that equal? Do the same with the width. Multiply the two figures to find out how many tiles you will need. Vinyl tile is sold by the box, so you will have to round out your overall figure, depending upon the number of tiles that come in the box. Buy more than you need—usually one extra carton is enough—so that you will have some extra tiles on hand in the event of a mistake or for replacement, if necessary, later on.

Positioning Tile in a Room

Tile will look peculiar if it is not positioned correctly in the room. If you simply start along one wall and move across the room, you will probably have to cut the last row of tile, and this can make all the tiles appear off balance. It is best, therefore, to start in the center of the room and work out to the walls, to create a harmonious look. Tiles along the edges of the room will undoubtedly have to be cut, but the cuts will appear balanced in relation to the room.

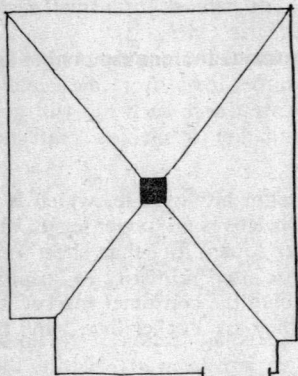

**Center First Tile;
OR Shift 45° on Center**

Finding the Center of the Room

Using two long strings, measure across the room from corner to corner, to create an X. Pushpin the two strings in place. Then, using a straightedge and a marker, follow each string as a guide and draw the X onto the floor. The intersection of the lines is the center of the room.

Lay the first tile exactly on the center. Decide if you want the tiles to run parallel with the walls or on the bias, which is a forty-five-degree angle.

Beginning to Draw a
Grid for the Tiles

If you want the tiles to be laid on the bias, which tends to look more balanced (especially if you are laying out a chckerboard pattern), turn the center tile forty-five degrees. Using it as a guide, take the straightedge and marker and draw out toward the corners on all four sides. You will now have drawn two parallel lines toward each corner, forming what is in essence a new double X. This X will not necessarily be the same shape as the first X, because the angle formed by the first X can be greater or less than forty-five degrees; it will only display the same angles if the room is square.

Measuring Off the Grid

Use a yardstick to measure off every 12″ along the double lines (or move one tile within these parallel lines) from the center of the floor to the corners, marking off where each tile will go as you proceed with a chalk pencil or marker (available at craft shops or your home center).

Installing the Tiles

Use the grid to lay out and install the tiles in the large X you created. Following the manufacturer's instructions and using a sawtoothed trowel, apply adhesive to the floor. Set the tile in adhesive and press firmly into place.

Once the X is in place, work on a small section of the floor at a time and proceed, tile by tile, toward the walls, butting them right up against each other. When you arrive at a wall, measure the uncovered floor and mark each tile to see how much you will have to cut off for it to fit. Cut off the excess with a sharp mat knife, then glue the adjusted tile in place.

Hard Floors Under Soft Coverings

For many homeowners and renters, hardwood and even ceramic tile floors are simply a background for a rug. Once the floor is in good shape, the decision must be made about what rug will look good in the room. Some people like to choose the rug before fabric; others wait until the fabric is selected before shopping for a rug. You will learn more about these options in the next chapter.

Some people prefer to cover their floors with wall-to-wall carpeting. This, of course, eliminates the hassle of refinishing the floor. It also provides a soft surface underfoot. A carpet can also be a pretty, neutral background for a rug.

To Recap

- Floors are a terrific investment. Well-finished wood floors will last for years.
- Damaged wood floors can be covered easily and quickly with new wood in popular strip, plank, or parquet styles.

- An old wood floor can be sanded and then refinished with a stain that replicates a wood tone, a pale pastel wash that looks like pickling, or paint.
- Paint can be enhanced by a faux finish, such as sponging, stippling, or stenciling.
- All wood finishes should be sealed and protected with polyurethane, a waterborne finish, or a paste wax.
- Some rooms, notably kitchens and baths, look wonderful with floors covered in ceramic tile or in sheet vinyl.
- Tile that's in good shape may only need to have its grout cleaned or replaced.
- The do-it-yourselfer can lay vinyl tile over an clean, flat, old floor using special adhesive.

PART THREE

Decorating Your Rooms

CHAPTER 6

Carpet and Rugs

Often called the fifth wall, the floor is both the easiest and the most problematic of surfaces to decorate. Easy, because the floor is usually a given in a house—sheathed in wood or tile, or covered in wall-to-wall carpet. And problematic to many because, if you are going to select a rug to cover part of a floor or layer upon a carpet, you must consider color, texture, and pattern just as you would in the selection of fabrics for your decorating scheme.

Carpet as a Preference

When they construct new housing, many home builders install wall-to-wall carpet in every room but the kitchen and baths (and entryway, often) because carpet is more economical than hardwood and it can be installed over a plywood subfloor. (They are responding to demand, too; according to industry studies, over three-quarters of Americans prefer wall-to-wall carpeting in their living rooms and bedrooms.) If you are moving into a new house and are working directly with its builder, you should be able to choose your carpet. (You can request a hardwood floor, but it will cost extra.)

Considering Carpet

When you look at carpet for a new home, remember that rooms lead and open from one to the next. It is safest to choose a single, neutral color, such as beige, taupe, or gray, that can travel throughout the space, without breaking the transition. A single color will unify the spaces and will make the rooms appear larger, too.

Another point to consider is durability. The traffic lanes traveled from room to room will also create pathways across the carpet. You will want to choose a durable carpet that will resist crushing and soiling in these areas.

A third consideration is upkeep. Dust settles on and in carpet, so it requires regular vacuuming and periodic deep cleaning. If you are prone to allergies, you may not be able to live with carpet; in this case, it is better to decorate with small area rugs or leave floors bare.

Fiber Choices

Traditionally, carpet was woven on a loom from wool. Wool is a natural fiber and it is exceedingly durable. Because of the time-consuming process of gathering wool and transforming it into yarn, the resulting fiber is far more expensive than man-made fibers such as nylon. Wool is vulnerable to moths and mildew. Wool carpet is usually made to order through the services of architects and designers who act as intermediaries to the manufacturers or mills.

Over 90 percent of all carpet sold in the United States is made of nylon. Nylon is very durable and reasonably priced. Nylon holds its color well, is easy to clean and, because it is synthetic, will not attract moths or mildew. Nylon comes under a variety of trade names including Anso IV and Stainmaster. The latter signifies that the carpet has been treated or protected against stains, soils, and spills.

Acrylic, a woollike synthetic, is used mostly in offices and other commercial installations. Two trade names for acrylic are Acrilan and Orlon.

A less often used man-made fiber is olefin, a mildew- and stain-resistant synthetic specified for indoor/outdoor carpet, especially in humid climates. Olefin resists static electricity. The most well-known trademarked olefin is Astroturf.

More well-known as an apparel fabric, polyester, a soft inexpensive alternative to nylon, is offered under several trade names including Dacron and Trevira. Polyester is extremely colorfast, but it tends to pill like a sweater, and it is not as durable as nylon.

Carpet manufacturers may blend two or more fibers to maximize the benefits of each. In other words, polyester, which is soft and colorfast, may be blended with nylon which is more durable and easy to clean.

Carpet Construction

Rugs were also hand-woven of wool, traditionally; many were hand-knotted, that is, individual strands were pulled through a backing and tied into knots. Some types of carpet, including Axminsters and Wiltons, are still mechanically woven.

Because carpet was made on wider looms than hand-knotted rugs, it was dubbed broadloom.

Over 90 precent of American-made nylon carpet is tufted, not woven; high-speed machines employ hundreds of needles to stitch loops of tightly twisted yarn through a woven synthetic fabric backing; a layer of latex locks the loops in place.

Loops stand upright. Sometimes the loops are left as is; sometimes the tops of the loops are sheared off to create a soft, even, plushy surface. This is called pile or cut pile.

Testing for Durability

The durability of carpet depends upon its texture and density, as well as on its fiber and the twist, or set, of the yarn. Generally speaking, the heavier the yarn, and the more tufts per square inch, the more durable the carpet.

The yarn should be tightly twisted. It might be slightly curled as well. To test for durability, bend the carpet back on itself; it should be difficult to bend. If you can see the backing—called the grin—this may indicate that the carpet is loosely woven and therefore not very durable. Check to see that none of the strands of yarn have snagged or pulled loose from the backing. Sometimes these can be snipped off, but they can also pull out altogether and leave a gap.

Loop and Pile

There are a number of variations on the loop and on pile. In general, level loop and level pile (both of which display an even surface) suit more formal settings, while multilevel surfaces, which play off low and high pile (or loops) in different so-called sculptured patterns, are more appropriate for informal situations.

When densely tufted, loop tends to be more hardy than pile because tightly packed loops are virtually impenetrable. Therefore, the carpet soils less readily and cannot be crushed or worn down as easily.

TYPES OF LOOP AND PILE

Level loop	Tufts are of an even height.
Multilevel loop	Tufts are pushed through at different heights. The surface appears sculptured.
Cut loop	The higher-level tufts are cut or sheared; the lower level tufts remain looped.
Random shear or tip shear	Tufts are all of a level, but some are cut or sheared and some are left as loops. The surface has a distinct yet soft textural appearance.
Frieze or twist	Also called *trackless* because the carpet masks footprints; curled or twisted tufts are looped.
Saxony plush or velvet	Tufts are sheared or cut all at the same level, usually ½″ or less, and they are densely packed.
Textured plush	Tufts are cut higher, or thicker—over ½″—and are not as densely packed.

Berber Carpet

One type of tight level loop and neutral-toned carpet—called Berber—is extremely durable, so it is often used in commercial spaces such as offices. For home use, Berbers treated with a soil repellent work well in high-traffic areas such as family rooms, home offices, and children's rooms.

Padding

All carpeting should be installed with padding or, as it is known in the profession, *underlay*. Like a box spring for a mattress, the underlay provides support for the carpet. Because the padding absorbs foot traffic and prevents the carpet from stretching or wrinkling, it also enhances the life of the carpet. Padding is a good insulator, too.

Saxony Plush

Frieze or Twist

Cut Loop

Level Loop

Padding, available in urethane, foam rubber, or a felt made of hair and jute, is manufactured in a variety of thicknesses and weights; it is often textured like a waffle to prevent slipping. The retailer who sells carpet will recommend the best padding for the carpet you select.

Viewing Carpet Samples

In the carpet showroom or floor-covering area of a department store or home center, large, doormat-size samples are typically displayed in waterfalls, which can be flipped so you can see and touch both the front and back of each sample. Small swatch-size pieces may also be available, either singly or glued on cards. The cards exhibit the color possibilities within one textural grouping.

You should be able to borrow samples of carpet to view at home. It is a good idea to do so as carpet will look different under different types of light. Once carpet is installed, it is cumbersome to remove, so you want to know that the color you like will really go with your furnishings and fabrics.

Measuring for Carpet

When you purchase carpet, you must know the actual dimensions of your floors, in square feet or yards, so that the retailer can estimate the quantity you will need. Take a floor plan with you—with the length and width of the room marked on it—to help the retailer with the calculations. Mark dimensions of any irregularities such as jogs in the wall, alcoves, protrusions such as bookcases, or hearths.

Carpet runs in a variety of widths, from 9' to 18'. The width of the carpet will affect how much you order. Try to choose a carpet that is as wide or wider than your room; that way you can avoid having to piece the carpet together, and you will avoid having a seam. Even when carpet is expertly installed, a seam does not vanish completely, and a seam can attract dust, too.

Colors and Patterns

Pale-colored or neutral-toned carpet is usually the best—and safest—choice because it goes with virtually any fabric and will outlast fabric changes if you decide to alter your decorating scheme in the future.

If you are going to choose a color other than a neutral for your carpet, it is best to have it match as closely as possible one of the colors in the dominant fabric used in the room. Consider how much the room or rooms will be trafficked. Light colors visually expand a space; deeper tones look cozy underfoot.

A patterned carpet may take the brunt of traffic and add vibrance to a room. Patterns and visible textures such as oatmeal are good when you want to camouflage or mask a surface, or hide temporary soiling. Simple patterns, such as a crisscross trellis, a mini-dot, or pale speckle work with many fabric choices.

Other patterns, such as Victorian-style cabbage roses or jazzy geometrics may set the stage for a nostalgic look at the past. In these cases, the fabrics in the room should not fight with the carpet; in fact, they should probably be neutral. (We will look at fabric more closely in the next chapter.)

Installing Carpet

Because of its weight and bulk and the difficulty involved in cutting and fitting, carpeting is almost always installed by a professional.

In fact, the price tag usually includes installation; padding is extra but, as mentioned above, highly recommended.

To prepare for installation, you should thoroughly clean the floors to be covered and remove furniture from the room.

Once the padding is laid, the installer rolls out the carpet for the best appearance in the room. If the carpet is to run from one room to another, he will adjust it accordingly before making any cuts. Once the carpet is correctly positioned, it is stretched taut and nailed through thin wood strips to the floor. Seams are aligned so that they dissolve visually.

Rugs

The words *carpet* and *rug* signify a difference in size and method of installation. A carpet is generally far larger than a rug and is laid down and affixed wall-to-wall with tacks or staples; a rug, usually smaller in size, is bound, or finished off around its edge with thick stitching or with a fabric hem. A rug defines an area of a room and it is not attached to the floor.

Early Rugs

Rugs have been made since time immemorial. Initially, rugs were woven on portable looms. In the Middle and Far East, rugs were used as saddle blankets and saddlebags and, in cold weather, they could double as capes, tent accoutrements, or to protect the knees during prayer. In the West, rugs were used to cover tabletops, chests, and beds; some were hung on walls to keep away dampness and cold.

In Europe and America, as looms increased in size, rugs could be woven to cover larger and larger areas and became specifically associated with floors.

Today's Choices

Today's choice of rugs seems limitless. Rugs are still made by hand in many countries of the world; many machine-made rugs mimic or replicate their handmade (or antique) counterparts. A rug can be custom designed—at some expense—to complement a decor; some rug manufacturers have created designs to specifically marry with companion furniture fabrics, to take the guessing out of a coordinated decorating scheme.

SOME SPECIFIC TYPES OF RUGS

Aubusson	Inspired by antique, tapestrylike, flat-woven rugs originally made in France. Patterned with floral and scroll motifs and with center medallions. (Another, similar French-style rug is the Savonnerie.)
Braided	Associated with Americana, oval or circular rug fabricated from braids of narrow fabric strips.
Dhurrie	Flat-woven, reversible, and made in India, mainly of wool and sometimes of cotton. Prices vary, but most styles are very reasonable. Patterns range from geometric shapes to scattered flower petals on a field of color.
Hooked	Small, often pictorial rug handmade from strips of fabric punched through burlap backing.
Kilim	Geometrically patterned flat-woven version of an Oriental rug.
Needlepoint	Hand-stitched wool rug, backed with linenlike fabric. Patterns range from floral to pictorial motifs. Most prized needlepoints come from Portugal.
Persian and Oriental	A loose definition of an intricately patterned knotted pile rug from the Middle East and Asia Minor. Authentic rugs are antiques, highly prized, and costly. Imitated widely, in varying degrees of quality.
Rag	Usually woven into runners. Handwoven from strips of fabric crossed through loom's linen thread warp.
Sisal	One of a grasslike family of natural-colored, natural fibers (others include coir, from coconut; reed, a seagrass; raffia, another reed; and jute) adapted for rugs exhibiting a simple textural weave.
Tatami mat	Straw mat, bordered in black cloth, made in Japan.

Creating a Rug from Carpet

Like carpet, a rug may be flat-woven or exhibit a soft, plushy pile surface. If you like the look and feel of carpet but prefer not to completely cover your floor, you can have a rug made from carpet. This solution may be beneficial, too, if your room is an awkward size or shape and cannot accommodate a standard-size rug.

Take your floor plan, with its furniture arrangement drawn in position, so that you can work out the exact size rug you will need. A rule of thumb: All the furniture should sit comfortably upon the rug with a small margin of carpet visible all around. In other words, plan the rug so that the legs of your furniture do not extend beyond its perimeter.

The carpet retailer will have the carpet cut and bound or finished off with a hem to your specifications. If you are working through a designer showroom, you may consider other options, such as having a compatible border sewn around the rug for added decorative interest. The border can be in the same loop or pile family as the field of the rug, or it may be another texture altogether, such as a needlepoint.

Standard Sizes

Most manufactured rugs conform to specific sizes, which are based on a room-enhancing rectangle. The smallest of these, $2' \times 3'$, $3' \times 5'$, and $4' \times 6'$, look best when positioned to accentuate or offset an architectural detail, such as a hearth, or a specific piece of furniture, such as a bed. These sizes, obviously, also work best in a bathroom, powder room, small entry, or small, narrow hallway.

The most common area- and room-size rugs measure $6' \times 9'$, $8' \times 10'$, $9' \times 12'$, and $12' \times 15'$. Occasionally, you can find rugs that are even larger—as large as $15' \times 18'$. The size you select should relate to the placement and arrangement of furniture in the room.

Rug Rules

As mentioned above, it looks best when all the furnishings in a specific grouping stand comfortably upon the rug. When the back legs of a chair or love seat in a seating group drop off the rug, it often throws the furniture arrangement out of balance.

In a dining room, the rug should be large enough so that the chairs still remain on the rug when they are pulled back and away from the table. If your table has leaves, the rug should be roomy enough to accommodate the table's full-size setup.

In the master bedroom, an area rug looks best when the bed and its companion nightstands are on the rug. A separate dresser and other furnishings can stand upon the floor or share the rug if it is big enough.

In a Large Room

If a room is very large and embraces two or more furniture groupings, you may want to plan on defining each separate grouping with its own rug, even if the floor is already covered with a wall-to-wall carpet. In a large room, rugs break up the space and add a feeling of coziness. The rugs should either match or be compatible. Two or three Orientals, for instance, may share coloring but not match up by pattern; the colors will unite them as a group.

How Rugs Are Displayed in the Showroom

Rugs are displayed in a showroom or department store in a variety of ways. When a rug is suspended like a fabric panel, you can inspect it front and back.

Often, though, rugs are stacked like pancakes, so you have to flip through until you find a rug you like; the retailer will then remove the rug from the pile so that you can view it in its entirety. Some imported and antique rugs will be rolled, or folded and rolled. Obviously these must be flung out so you can see the entire pattern or design.

Checking on Patterns

Most rugs are patterned. You should take with you a sample of the fabric you are going to use in the room to compare the colors and the pattern so that you can coordinate the two. (If mixing patterns intimidates you, stick with a plain-colored rug such as a sisal or have a piece of carpet cut and bound for you.)

Some rugs, such as geometrically patterned dhurries and many Orientals, will coordinate with a wide variety of fabrics based on a color palette, even if the designs cannot match. Therefore, you can be quite creative and even daring in your choice.

Checking on Size

The rug you buy will affect the look of your room, so, once you have looked at a variety of choices and have zeroed in on the rug you prefer, you may want to rethink the size that will look best. In other words, the rug you like may work best if it virtually fills the room, except for a border at the baseboards, rather than just defines an area.

Many people, in fact, opt for a room-size rug, to take the guesswork out of their decision.

Also, a rug in the showroom will **always** look smaller than it will at home because the showroom itself is so large. If you are uncertain about how the rug ought to look, check to see if you can take it home on approval. Designer showrooms, established department stores, and decorator outlets allow this; some retailers do not.

Remember the Underlay

The life of a rug is enhanced by padding. An underlay will alleviate wear and tear, will cushion the rug, and will prevent the rug from slipping out from underfoot.

A rug underlay can be purchased precut, or you can buy it by the yard and cut it yourself. Most rug underlays are meshlike, made from a rubbery, latexlike material. If you want to cushion your rug even more, ask the retailer to cut a piece of carpet underlay for you.

If you feel cautious about slipping on a rug, you can lay down a special double-sided carpet tape along the edges. Press the rug firmly onto the tape to secure it. Add extra pieces at the corners because corners can become unglued and turn back, posing an obstacle to trip over.

Sometimes the decision about what rug you want will follow the decision about the fabric you prefer for your upholstery, window treatments, and table covers. If this is the case, read the chapter that follows, which will tell you all about choosing fabrics, and then return to this chapter.

To Recap

- Wall-to-wall carpet is a soft way to both define and visually warm up a room or link several rooms or spaces together.
- Choose a carpet not only for its appearance but for its durability.
- The texture of a carpet will make it look formal or casual.
- Carpet must be installed by a pro, and should be cushioned with padding to enhance its durability and life.
- Rugs can be considered as small versions of carpet or as separate, patterned elements in a decorating scheme.
- Rugs come in a range of sizes, from room-size to accent-size.
- Rugs come in a virtually unlimited range of patterns, so you should take a sample of the fabric you will use in the room with you when you go shopping to be sure your fabric and rug will harmonize.

CHAPTER 7

Fabrics

If you are purchasing a piece of upholstered furniture at retail, chances are you will be asked to choose your covering from a group of home furnishings fabrics preselected by the furniture manufacturer as those most suited to the piece. The fabrics are offered in a range of prices based upon the fiber content/blend, weave, and initial expense to the furniture manufacturer.

Inspecting the Floor Sample

Before looking these over, though, inspect the specific fabric covering the floor sample. You want to be certain that the overall workmanship of the piece will be to your liking, no matter what fabric you ultimately choose. Is the upholstery sufficiently thick and heavy so that it can endure years of wear? Does it fit smoothly over the piece, with no wrinkles? Are the seams taut and free of puckers? If the piece is trimmed with welting—a fabric-covered cord—is that welting straight? Are cushion zippers even? If there is a skirt, does it hang smooth and straight? Is it lined?

Is the platform or deck—the fabric stretched over the seat underneath the cushions—also thick and taut, even if it is a different fabric than the upholstery? Does the color of the deck fabric complement the upholstery fabric?

Position of the Fabric

Inspect the upholstery more closely. Is the fabric positioned correctly on the piece, i.e., is the pattern, if any, centered on the back and across the arms? Does it match across the seams, including across the places where the seat cushions meet the base of the piece and the skirt? In other words, does the pattern appear to travel in an unbroken line from the top of the back, across the seat cushions, and down the front of the base to the floor? It should.

If you are satisfied with the workmanship of the floor sample, you should be assured that the piece you order and eventually receive will be of good quality, too.

Before Committing to a Manufacturer's Fabric

If, after inspection, you decide you like the sofa or chair shown you, but want to work with a different fabric, ask to borrow (or buy) samples of several of the fabrics to see what they look like at home. Often a fabric—as well as paint chips, for example— will look surprisingly different because the lighting in a showroom, furniture store, or department store is usually stronger than that at home. Also, the store may be lit by fluorescents, and devoid of daylight. You should look at your samples both under lamplight and in daylight to see what looks best for your room. (You should take home a sample of fabric even if it is the same as shown on the floor sample, for the same reasons; it is better to be safe than sorry.)

Kinds of Fabric Samples

There are two kinds of samples. Memo samples are large enough (usually at least a foot square) to show the entire repeat or motif that is, indeed, repeated over the surface of the fabric. Swatches, which are also called cuttings, are little pieces you can use only to check for color.

Sometimes you can simply borrow memos. If so, you will be given a deadline for returning them, or you will have to pay for them anyway. If the store requires that you buy memos, you can usually deduct their price from the price of the piece you agree to purchase. You may want to buy one or two memos in any case, so you can refer to them when you make other purchases for your home, such as rugs. You can take away as many swatches as you like; these are free of charge.

Customer's Own Material

If, after deliberation, you decide you still like the piece but dislike the manufacturer's fabric selection, you may be able to independently seek out your own fabric, either at the store—if it has a larger selection—or at a fabric showroom or shop. In the trade, this is called C.O.M. or *customer's own material*. You will probably be charged a fee for working with it.

Checking Quality

Upholstery fabric must stand up to wear and tear, so it should be thick, heavy, and tightly woven. When you take home a memo, inspect it thoroughly. Hold the memo in your hands and tug it, straight across and also from corner to corner. The fabric should give, but not feel loose or floppy. Scratch the memo. None of the threads should come loose. Rub it with an eraser; a poor-quality fabric will pill—flecks of fabric will come off on the eraser.

Also check the fiber content. Natural fibers, such as cotton, linen, wool, and silk can be expensive. Each has its advantages and disadvantages (see chart following). Synthetics, used alone, also have disadvantages. It may be preferable to choose a fabric that has been blended from natural and synthetic fibers, to gain the best attributes of both.

Fiber Content

Because each fiber has its own special properties, fabric manufacturers often create blends to balance the advantages of both (as carpet manufacturers do). Sometimes the fabric blends two of the

Fiber	Type	Strength	Colorfastness	Susceptible to	Resists
Cotton	Natural	Moderately strong, firm, absorbent, pliable, soft	Good to excellent	Sunlight—may yellow and/or fade, mildew, shrinking	Abrasion, static electricity
Linen	Natural	Strong, firm, absorbent, pliable, lustrous	Good to excellent	Wrinkling	Abrasion, fading, mildew, moths
Silk	Natural	Strong, pliable	Good	Sunlight, bleeding	Wrinkling, mildew, moths
Wool	Natural	Very strong, absorbent, pliable, elastic	Good to excellent	Moths, mildew, shrinking, pilling	Abrasion, fading, wrinkling
Rayon	Natural	Moderately strong, pliable, soft, lustrous	Good	Abrasion, mildew, wrinkling, shrinking	
Acrylic	Synthetic	Strong, resembles wool, pliable	Good to excellent		Fading, wrinkling, shrinking, mildew, moths
Nylon	Synthetic	Very strong, silky, pliable, elastic	Good	Sunlight, static electricity, pilling, soils	Abrasion, wrinkling, mildew, moths
Polyester	Synthetic	Strong, cottonlike	Good to excellent	May yellow, static electricity, pilling, lint, soils	Abrasion, wrinkling, shrinking, moths, stains
Polypropylene (olefin)	Synthetic	Very strong, not very pliable, lustrous	Good		Moisture, mildew, stains

same type fiber, such as two naturals—cotton with linen—for the same reason. Look at the label to determine whether or not the fabric you like is a blend, and in what proportion. Many sheeting companies, for example, blend cotton and polyester in a 50/50 ratio, or in a 35/65 ratio.

Fabric Types

Even when you understand the properties of the various fibers, it's good to get to know some of the home furnishings fabrics you can choose that are suitable for upholstery.

(There are home furnishings fabrics that are not durable enough for upholstery. These fabrics—especially thin, loosely woven cottons or blends—may be fine for curtains, bedspreads, or tablecloths.)

Broadcloth	Usually cotton; lustrous and tightly woven with ribs that follow the weft, or length of the fabric, like grain in wood.
Brocade	Usually cotton or rayon, and/or expensive silk. The term refers to an all-over tone-on-tone raised pattern that resembles embroidery.
Canvas	Heavyweight and tightly woven, usually in cotton or linen; comes in various weights. A lighter weight canvas is called *duck;* medium weight, *sailcloth*.
Chintz	Thin, finely woven cotton that is usually glazed and printed in a pattern; often in a floral or leafy motif. Heavy, unglazed, unprinted chintz is also called *cretonne*.
Corduroy	Finely woven, heavy cotton with raised, velvety ribs that range from very fine to thick.
Damask	Lustrous, finely woven, usually of cotton or silk, but can be linen or rayon. Pattern is matte on face and shiny on the reverse side.
Homespun	Refers more to coarse, loosely woven, slightly nubby texture; cotton or linen, often striped or checked.
Muslin	Thin, loosely woven, fairly coarse cotton. Often used as the material for an undercover, under upholstery, which adds to the durability of a piece. Blended with polyester for sheeting.
Percale	Refers to smooth, finely woven sheeting, usually in a blend of cotton and polyester.
Ticking	Usually a heavy, firm, and finely woven cotton or linen; usually striped, and most often used to cover mattresses and bed pillows.

Reading the Label on a Fabric Sample

You will find the fiber content described on a label sewn or stapled onto the memo or swatch. Knowing fiber content is important, because certain fibers, such as 100 percent cotton, or a 50/50 cotton/linen blend, work better for upholstery or slipcovers; others, such as silk, may be too delicate, except for use on side chairs, for instance, that may not be sat upon as often, or for draperies.

Besides fiber content, you will learn other characteristics of the fabric, such as its repeat, its width, and its dominant color, or *colorway*. The pattern will be indicated by a number and possibly by a name as well. The fabric manufacturer may be named unless the retail outlet places its logo on the sample instead.

If you like the pattern of the memo you take home, but you do not like the colorway, chances are there are other colorways to choose from. Ask. Some plain fabrics such as cotton canvas or glazed cotton come in a veritable rainbow of hues—as many as three dozen, or more.

Fabric Widths

Most American fabrics made for home furnishings measure 54″ wide, although they can range from 45″ or 48″ to 60″ in width. European fabrics tend to be narrower, while specialty fabrics (such as theatrical gauze, which is often used for curtains, can be far wider—up to 100″ wide or more).

The wider the fabric, the less yardage you will need overall to upholster a piece of furniture, because fewer pieces of fabric will have to be sewn together to cover it. Be sure you take the width of the fabric into account when you calculate your yardage needs with your salesperson.

Regarding Repeats

The repeat of a pattern, as mentioned previously, indicates one full design or motif that is then reiterated over and over along the fabric. The larger the repeat, the more fabric you will need to cover your sofa, love seat, or chair. Why? Because, to look right, the pieces of fabric have to be adjusted to match across the seams and this can consume extra yardage if the repeat is large. There will be leftover fabric.

Save this fabric for extra arm caps. Arm caps are slipped over the arms of a piece to protect them from wear and tear; arm caps may also wear out, but they are easy to replace, whereas the arms themselves would have to be reupholstered.

Conversely, a mini-print or plain fabric will have no repeat, so there will be little waste.

Railroading versus Right Way

If the fabric is plain or the mini-print is tiny and nondirectional, the upholsterer can save even more fabric by running it the length of the piece, rather than from top to bottom. This is called *railroading*. Railroading does not effect the overall appearance of the piece.

If the repeat of the print is greater than six inches, or has an obvious directional appearance, the fabric will have to be stretched and cut from back to front, top to bottom, over and across the piece in the method known as *right way*. The larger the piece of furniture, the greater the likelihood of seaming and, therefore, the greater the need to be sure there is adequate yardage to accommodate matching up repeats across the seams.

Considering Fabric Care

Finally, before selecting a fabric, consider how easily it can be cleaned. Many home furnishings fabrics are treated with a soil repellent that prolongs the life of the fabric. The coating may also resist moisture and stains. It may be flame retardant, too. Check.

If the cushions have zippered upholstery covers, find out if they can be cleaned, and how. Will they shrink if cleaned? Can the covers be washed, or must they be dry cleaned? An unglazed cotton, for example, might be able to be washed; a wool or silk must be dry cleaned. Check.

You should also check to see if cleaning will affect colorfastness. Will the fabric fade when cleaned? Will it fade in direct sunlight, too? Natural fibers tend to fade over time, while synthetics tend to hold color longer. A natural/synthetic blend fabric should retain its color better than a natural one. What is your preference? Some people like a faded look; others want the bright, crisp appearance of their chosen fabric to last indefinitely.

A note of caution: Never remove inner cushion covers for cleaning. These hold the cushion filling in place.

Soil Repellents

If the fabric is treated with a soil repellent, will this finish dissolve with cleaning? Check your dry cleaners to see if they can revive the coating. If you want to refresh the repellent yourself, spray applications are available, too, though these tend to be somewhat less effective than the original coating because they do not penetrate as deeply.

Fabric Color

Once all is said and done, we arrive, full circle again, at the appearance of the fabric, and how the fabric will complement the rest of your decor.

If you take memos home with you, you should be able to tell whether or not the fabric you like will work well, but are there any hard-and-fast rules to follow?

Not really. Because a sofa is so large, it may be best to consider a color and a pattern that is not too overpowering. A sofa will dominate the room it is in, no matter what, so you may want to subdue its presence. For many years, people preferred having all fabrics match in a room (much in the same way that they liked having all their dishes match in a table setting), and so the same fabric used on the seating was teamed with that used at the windows. Today this is less apt to happen because people seem to like to mix and match, or coordinate patterns more than they used to.

Testing Colors

Decorators often create what they call *boards* to visualize how the various elements of a room will go together. You might want to try this, too. You can cut a board from any piece of thick cardboard or paper. First, glue down the paint chip indicating the color of the walls (if any); then arrange swatches of the various fabrics you are considering on the board next to the chip.

How many different fabrics do you want in the room? One rule of thumb is: three major fabrics, one for the sofa and, possibly, a complementary easy chair; one for other upholstered seating; one for the window treatments. If you feel quite daring, you may add even more fabrics for pillows, a footstool, and lampshades.

On the other hand, if you feel less than enthusiastic about the pattern-on-pattern, eclectic look, then stick with one or two fabrics for your major pieces. In this case, you may want a neutral or plain tone for your sofa. Remember that a beige will require a great deal of upkeep. If you prefer neutrals, you may want to look at deeper tones such as taupe or grayed greens. If you like color, choose one from a patterned fabric you plan on using elsewhere in the room or from your rug.

Dye Lots

Whatever color and pattern you choose, ask that all of the yardage you will need come from the same dye lot. No matter how they try, fabric manufacturers cannot guarantee that one batch of dye will replicate another precisely; there often is a variation in tone from one dye lot to the next. If you can, ask to see a sample of your fabric before it is cut for your piece.

Texture and Weave

Some fabrics look better as upholstery than others. Besides color and pattern, you should consider texture, too.

If you are going to work with a plain color or a mini-print, you may want to add visual interest to your selection with texture. The simplest texture is a plain over-under, linen weave. As implied, this weave is common to linen. It is also indicative of a canvas and chintz.

A small, repeated, all-over pattern in a weave is known as a *dobby;* a diagonal rib is called a *twill;* rep cloth has ribs that run with the grain.

Some Popular Patterns

Besides chintzes, which are usually florals varying from bud to bouquet, there are a wide variety of patterns to consider for upholstery.

Heavyweight cotton damask is often used for upholstery. Damasks are usually one color; as mentioned previously on the fabric chart, the design on the fabric is created by combining a number of weave designs which play dark and light tones off against each other.

Paisleys are multicolored patterns based on a motif that looks a bit like a large comma or teardrop, which is itself based on a stylized plant form; the teardrops are evenly spaced over the surface of the fabric.

The most basic geometric pattern is the stripe; stripes range from hairline thin to several inches thick; the latter are called awning stripes because they are, indeed, used so often on awnings. Another favorite geometric pattern is the check.

Mixing Patterns

When you work with a number of different patterns, it is best to mix one large-scale pattern with less obtrusive ones. Many fabric manufacturers purposely create *collections,* or coordinated ensembles, to take the guesswork out of the mix. Often a large-scale pattern will be teamed with a stripe and with a variety of small patterns, including one or two tiny, overall, nondirectional patterns, as well as with a broad range of plain fabrics in compatible colors.

If you can obtain a sample of the large-scale patterned fabric showing its selvages—the finished edges running along its width—you might be lucky enough to see a series of color dots displayed. These indicate the colors present in the pattern and, obviously, the colors compatible with that pattern.

Trimmings

You can have fun with trim. Usually, a piece of upholstered furniture will be trimmed with a self-welt, cord covered in fabric that matches the upholstery. You may want to specify a welt in a contrasting hue, you may not want any welting at all, or you may want a wider welt or even a double welt.

. If you really want to splurge, you may want to replace the skirt on your sofa or chair with fringe. Or, you may ask if the skirt could be accented with a contrasting grosgrain ribbon along the hem.

Skirt Styles

One of the options open to you when you upholster is the type of skirt, if any, you would like on your piece. If you do not request a special skirt treatment, it probably will be tailored with a simple pleat—called a tuxedo pleat—at the corners, plus another pleat at the center front seam. A variation on the tuxedo is the box pleat, which continues all the way around the piece.

Variations on corner treatments include a double pleat and a gathered insert. If the fabric you choose is soft enough, you can ask that the entire skirt be ruffled or gathered.

Skirt Drop

Usually the skirt falls—or drops—to the floor from a point about halfway down the base of the sofa or easy chair. If you like, you might be able to request that the skirt drop directly from the deck, just under the seat cushions.

A long skirt looks fuller than a short one, especially if it is gathered. Be sure that it will look right in proportion to the back and sides of the piece before specifying it. The length of the skirt should not exceed the height of the back or the piece of furniture will appear bottom-heavy.

Slipcovering Upholstered Furniture

Because a sofa, love seat, chaise, or easy chair can cost a substantial amount of money, it should last a long time—even a lifetime. For this reason, many people elect to cover a favorite piece once it appears to be wearing out. Others choose to put slipcovers over their existing upholstery for a seasonal change of decor. Still others want to protect their investment from the accidental spills and stains that are part and parcel of everyday, informal activity, stripping off the covers only when they entertain.

The Slipcover Option

These days, many furniture manufacturers offer the option of ordering a complementary slipcover at the time of purchase. This decision stands the customer in good stead, whatever the outlook for wear and tear. Even if the slipcover is not put on immediately, it can be saved for the future.

The Slipcover Advantage

Not only does a slipcover protect upholstery, it can be maintained more easily. A slipcover can be removed for cleaning and put right back on the piece. Slipcovering is also a wonderful way to dress up a piece of old furniture that may have been given to you or that you purchased at an estate sale or flea market.

Slipcover Fabrics

Because a slipcover is supposed to be taken on and off with ease, the fabric should be softer and more pliable than the standard upholstery-weight fabric. Lightweight canvas duck and chintz are very popular because they are both sturdy and easy to care for. Linen is another choice, but it wrinkles easily. For a more formal look, a lightweight damask is an option.

The Sheet Option

A truly economical fabric is sheeting. Yard for yard, sheets are the least expensive fabric you can buy and that is why so many decorating magazines suggest you consider sheets if you do not have a great deal of money to spend. Sheets are washable, too, which many slipcover fabrics are not; you can pop a slipcover made from sheets right in the washer and dryer and put it back on the piece of furniture as easily as you would put a fitted sheet on a bed. The one disadvantage is the fact that sheets are quite transparent, and so they will not work as a cover for a dark piece of furniture or for one with a bold pattern that would show through.

Getting a Slipcover Made Professionally

Unless you are very talented with a needle and thread, you will probably have a slipcover made by a professional. A slipcover is a bulky item and requires skill, especially when inserting industrial-weight zippers or Velcro for a correct fit. Slipcovers are made by upholsterers who are listed as such in the Yellow Pages. Home decorating centers often have a team of freelance artisans on file or in their employ; these pros work on the assumption that you will purchase your fabric from the store.

The Slipcover House Call

Many upholsterers make house calls, or give at-home estimates based on the fabric you choose, the amount of yardage needed, and the labor involved, especially if you want to add a specialty trim. Usually, they stock an extensive selection of fabrics appropriate for slipcovers, so you can make your choice on the spot. If you want to supply your own fabric, there may be a surcharge because the upholsterer hopes to make a percentage of the fee from the fabric sold.

Once you have made your selection, the upholsterer will bring the fabric to your home and will cut it directly on the piece. The slipcover will be sewn at the factory, returned, and fitted on the piece for you. You can request that the piece be taken away and returned when ready, but this is not necessary.

Once walls and ceilings are painted and floors prepared, you are ready to furnish your rooms. All anyone really needs for day-to-day comfort is a place to lounge or sit, a place to eat and do projects, a place to sleep, and places for storage. The first priority is a comfortable place to sit. For this reason—and because we just looked at fabrics—we will turn next to upholstered furniture and look at how it is made so you can make an informed choice when you purchase pieces for your home.

To Recap

- Inspect fabric on any furniture floor sample before making your own selection. Be sure it looks right on the piece and fits snugly, with no puckers or wrinkles.
- Take home fabric samples to "eye test" them in your room.
- Pull, tug, and scratch fabric to be sure it is durable.
- Consider how you will take care of the fabric once it is on the piece of furniture.
- Choose a fabric pattern and color you will want to live with.
- Sometimes the upholstered piece can be customized to your liking; check to see if there are any options you can choose from, such as a trimming or skirt style. Some upholstered pieces come with extra pillows, too. Ask.
- Consider a slipcover if you already own upholstered furniture, or add one for a change of mood, or to change with the season.

CHAPTER 8

Upholstery

The furniture you will use over and over is the furniture you should spend the most on. Unless this is your first home and you plan on trading up later on, invest in the best-quality upholstered furniture if you can, at least for the rooms you will use most often. The extra money you spend on a well-constructed, well-padded, and tautly covered easy chair, sofa, or love seat—or all three—will be worth it in the long term.

Where to Buy Upholstered Furniture

Furniture is sold in a number of venues. The most common are department stores, furniture stores, or galleries. Furniture can also be bought in "one-stop" shops or franchises owned and operated by an individual manufacturer or marketer; these outlets literally provide everything you may want, from a sofa to lamps to framed art for the walls.

Purchasing Furniture by Mail

You can order furniture by mail, but you have to trust the catalog's photograph and description. A photograph may be deceptive in depicting true colors and textures. A photograph cannot vouch for the quality of the construction of a piece, either.

If you go this route, you should find out the returns policy in case you do not like your selection. Usually, the piece must be sent back in its original wrapping or container. If you can, you should unpack and inspect the piece while the delivery truck is at your house; that way, you can put it right back on the truck if it is damaged or if it does not match up with what you expected from the catalog description.

Looking Beneath the Surface

Just as you cannot tell a book by its cover, so, too, can you be distracted from the underlying workmanship—or construction—of a sofa or chair by its fabric covering. The first impression matters, of course, because shape and style will determine how the piece will look in your room; but remember that you usually can select an alternate covering if you do not like the fabric on the sample you are shown.

A First Test

Before you check the construction of the upholstered piece that appeals to you, do give it a general check to see if it suits and fits your body. Sit in the piece. Is it deep enough, or too deep? If it is deep, will additional pillows make you feel better? Is the height of the seat comfortable? Does the pitch—the angle—of the back feel right?

Bounce on it. Does the seat cushion give? You should feel no lumps. You should hear no squeak, either, for this indicates faulty springs. The frame should not wobble or creak.

Components of Construction

Almost every piece of upholstered furniture comprises four components: frame (usually wood, but occasionally metal); springs (unless it is an all-foam piece); padding (which envelops the structural elements), and fabric.

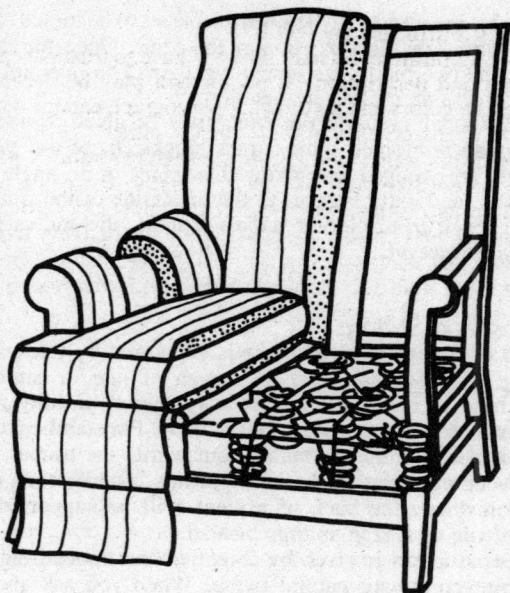

Anatomy of an Upholstered Chair

The Frame

Once you have eyeballed your favorite piece, ask the salesperson to tell you what wood the frame is made of and ask him or her to have the piece tipped back so that you can inspect it thoroughly.

The best kind of frame is made of a smoothly finished, kiln-dried hardwood such as hickory, maple, or elm—the thicker the better. Ask the salesperson if the frame on the piece you like is made of one of these woods. If the wood is not kiln-dried, it may shrink and warp over time. If the wood is not smooth, it may splinter or crack.

Both pairs of legs, front and back, should be of equal thickness. Heavier pieces have braces called stretchers that link the legs from back to front and from side to side for extra support. The stretchers look like an H.

All joints should be strong. The strongest joints are doweled (or double-doweled). Dowels are thin, cylindrical, pluglike pieces of wood that are inserted in holes in the pieces to be joined together; once in place, the dowels support the joint. Once the dowel is inserted, the two pieces are joined together. You may not see the dowels, unless their ends are visible.

For additional strength, the joints may be glued. Some pieces may also be reinforced with corner blocks; these are pieces of wood that are wedged and screwed in place at an angle behind the joint to lend extra support to the underside of the frame.

If you see drips of glue or staples or nails, this indicates poor-quality construction.

Webbing and Springs

The seat of the upholstered piece is supported by thick strips of webbing. The webbing may be woven of jute, a natural fiber usually used to make rope, or of a synthetic—usually polypropylene, which resists moisture and mildew. For stability, the webbing should be tightly woven and taut within the frame.

The webbing forms the base for springs, usually coils made of steel. Sometimes the back of a piece will be supported by so-called *no-sag* or zigzag springs instead.

The best support is given by coils tied and knotted eight ways to adjacent coils with natural twine. When you ask about construction, you should ascertain if there are twenty-four coils per seat, the best number to ensure comfort and durability.

Padding

The frame, webbing, and springs must be padded so that you do not feel them through the upholstery. If you press against any part of the piece and feel the outline of the springs, that indicates poor-quality construction. Another no-no are lumps. The padding should feel smooth across the entire piece.

Traditionally, padding was made from horsehair or from cotton batting. These days, it will most likely be made of polyester fiberfill, and, less often, from foam. If the padding is constructed in layers, the top layer may be made of down or a feather-and-down mix sandwiched and quilted between two layers of fabric.

In fine-quality upholstered pieces, the entire padded frame is wrapped in muslin, both to secure the padding and as an undercover for the fabric used to upholster the piece.

Cushions

A sofa (or chair) will undoubtedly have seat cushions; many have back cushions, too. You should check the construction of these as carefully as you do the frame. Each cushion should bear a tag that tells you what it is filled with. For maximum comfort, the back and seat cushions should feel about the same. In other words, firm back cushions should be paired with firm seat cushions. If one set is firm and the other is soft, you will not feel as comfortable. You will feel as if you are sinking back too far if the back cushions are soft and the seat cushions are hard—and vice versa.

Cushion Fillings
The firmest cushions are made of dense polyurethane foam, of polyester fiberfill, or of individually encased and padded steel coils. The softest are filled with goose down, which many interior designers prefer. Other options include feathers over foam (or fiberfill) and down over springs.

When you purchase a sofa or chair, you may be able to specify or select the content of its cushions. Ask the salesperson to describe your options. Your main consideration will be firmness. How far do you want to sink into your sofa or chair? Look also to see if—and how quickly—the cushions reassume their original shape. Will you have to fluff them up every time you sit on them?

Cushion Shape and Appearance
Each cushion should conform to and fit snugly within the upholstered frame. Seat cushions should not protrude but should fit flush with the front of the piece. The arms of the piece will dictate the silhouette of the seat cushion. If the arms are set back, a cushion will extend in front of each. A chair that requires a single cushion will take on a T configuration. A multicushioned love seat or sofa will require two L-shaped cushions plus one or two additional square or rectangular ones in the middle if the sofa is extra long.

The cushions should be thick and should feel—and give—the same on both sides so that you can flip or reverse them. Sit on both sides of the seat cushions and lean against both sides of the back cushions, if any, to be sure there are no lumps in the filling.

For maintenance purposes, the cushions should be covered in muslin (or ticking) so that their upholstered covers can be removed for cleaning. Upholstery zippers should be even and straight, with

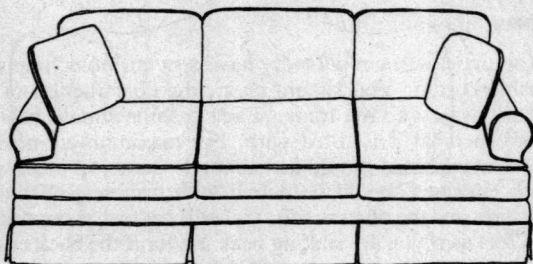

**Pillowback Sofa with
Lawson Arm and Tuxedo Pleat Skirt**

no puckers. There should be no puckering along the seams of the covers, either.

The Shape of the Sofa or Chair

After all this discussion about construction, we arrive, full circle, right where we started—with how a sofa or love seat or chair looks. A sofa, love seat, or easy chair generally will assume one of a handful of predetermined shapes. In addition, you may be able to ask for a specific type of arm or leg without incurring any extra expense.

BACKS

Club or pillowback	Exhibits a plain, relatively chubby silhouette, with a straight-across back fitted with pillows and arms that are lower than the back.
Camelback or serpentine	Based on eighteenth-century designs. The arms slope or "ride" slightly from the back, depending upon the curve and sweep of the back, and curl outward. The back may have more than one curve or "hump." An Americana variation, with centered double curve, is the *heart back*.
Chesterfield	A cross between a club and a tuxedo, with buttons punctuating the upholstery; may be called a *tufted back*.

**Camelback Love Seat
with Marlborough Leg**

Tuxedo	Displays a straight, squared profile, with arms that are a continuation of the back, both in height and usually in thickness, too.

Legs and Feet

If you decide not to skirt the sofa or easy chair, you may be able to specify a preference in leg or foot.

Cabriole or Queen Anne	Based on an eighteenth-century design. Double-curved, tapering leg, usually terminates in a pad foot, which is a flat, ovoid foot raised on a disclike base.
Marlborough	A straight, square leg, sometimes grooved with fluting—narrow, vertical semicircular channels; usually terminates in a boxlike, squared-off foot.
Parsons	A thick variation on the Marlborough; usually upholstered. A variation is the *shell* leg, which tapers slightly from the base of the piece. No foot.
Ball or bun	Can be made of wood or upholstered. May support the seat directly, or be the termination of a leg. An antique variation is the claw and ball (literally an eaglelike claw grasping a ball).

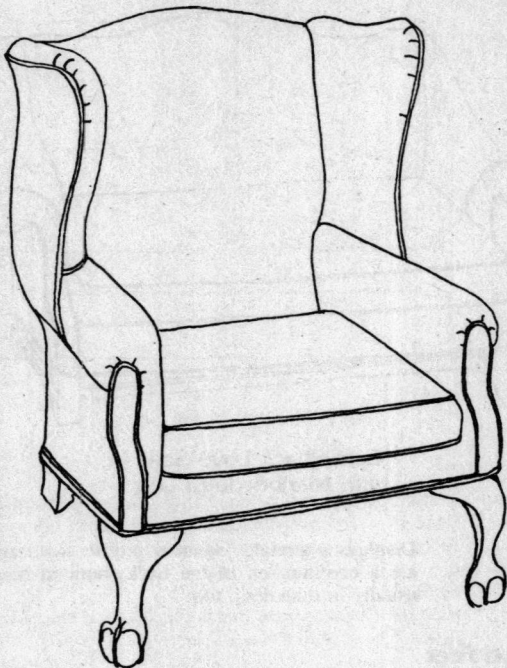

Wing Chair with Ball and Claw Foot

Arms

When you order a sofa, love seat, or chair, you may be able to specify the style of arm as well.

English The front of the arm is slightly higher than the back, and it rolls slightly outward, too; pleated where the arm turns down to the base.

Lawson Slightly curved arm; variations include a pleated or *waterfall pleat* arm, which often fans pleats from a tuft or button; a shorter, thicker Lawson is the *sock* arm.

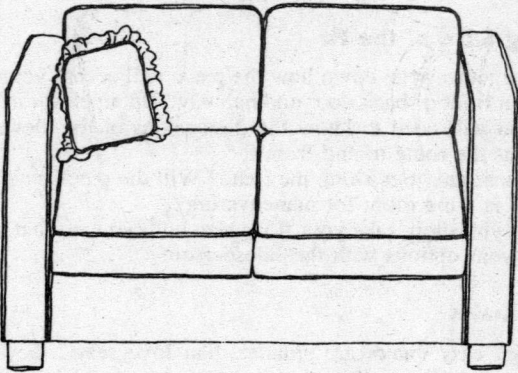

Tuxedo Arm Love Seat

Saddlebag	Contemporary, pillowlike arm resting on a straight upright, Tuxedo-style frame; often used for leather upholstery.
Scroll	Exaggerated, narrow roll; if the arm is divided with a seam, the scroll is rolled over the upright frame and is called a *rolled* arm.
Tuxedo	Extends directly from a straight back; if the tuxedo drops down, it is called a *track* arm.

Sofa and Love Seat Sizes

A love seat typically measures 54″, 60″, or 72″ in length; a sofa is longer, as much as 96″ long (and even longer if you custom order). If you want an even grander seating arrangement, you will probably have to create your own configuration with sectional pieces.

The depth and height of a love seat or sofa will vary, too. Before finalizing your decision, you should take into account not only the dimensions of the piece (or pieces) you are purchasing but also the width of the doorways the piece will have to squeeze through, as well as the width of the wall it will rest against, if this is part of your design scheme.

Making Sure of the Fit

Don't forget to write down how the piece will access your house: through a front or back door and hallway? Up an elevator? In this case, you will need to know the dimensions of the elevator cab as well as the route to and from it.

Are there any jogs along the route? Will the piece have to turn corners? Is there room for maneuvering?

When you shop, take your floor plan with you, so that you can discuss your options with the salesperson.

Easy Chairs

Although easy chairs are smaller than love seats, they can be surprisingly bulky and should, therefore, be measured in the same

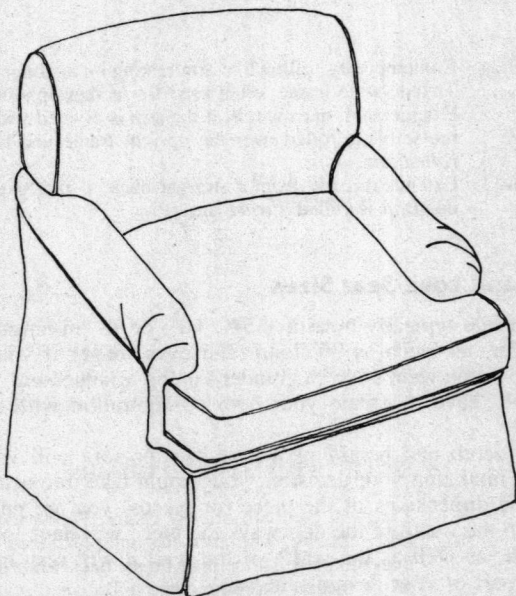

Club Chair

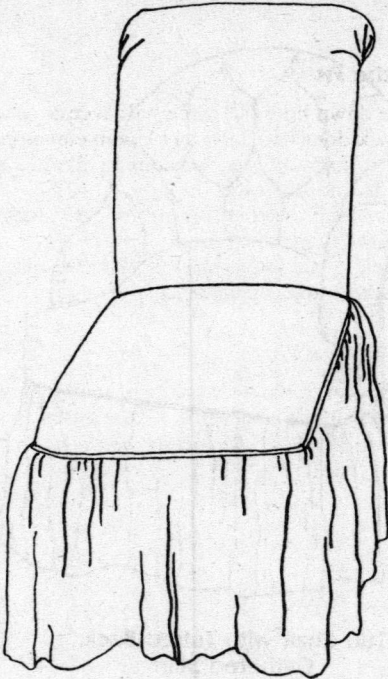

Slipper Chair

way as their larger counterparts. A wing chair, for example, has a high back and can be very deep in the seat, which makes it awkward to maneuver through a doorway or around a tight corner. A club or tub chair may be easier to handle. Consult your floor plan and your salesperson before committing to a specific easy chair.

TYPES OF UPHOLSTERED CHAIRS

Club   The most common of easy chairs. Well-padded, fairly chubby, with arms that are positioned lower than the back. Arms may be set back from the front of the piece to accommodate a T-shaped seat cushion.

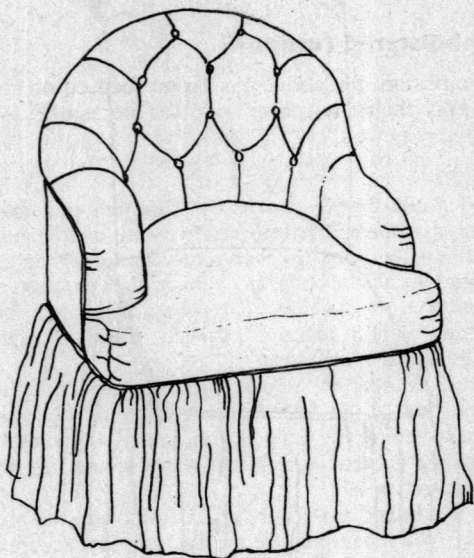

**Tub Chair with Tufted Back,
Gathered Skirt**

Fauteuil and bergere	Only partially upholstered; the frame is exposed and outlines the upholstery. A fauteuil's arms are completely filled in with upholstery to match the back, whereas a bergere's are open and padded only on top—as comfortable armrests.
Slipper	Small, armless, usually short-legged chair, often relegated to the bedroom; may or may not have a separate seat cushion.
Tub	Back and arms of the tub chair form one continuous curve; often tufted for visual interest.
Wing	Historically developed as an antidote to drafts; wings situated between back and arms protected the sitter. Legs normally exposed; back and arms may reveal exposed frames as well.

Other Upholstered Furniture

To resist confusion, the above discussion focused on sofas, love seats, and easy chairs, but there are other pieces of furniture that are upholstered as well.

Sofa Bed

Also called a convertible couch, the sofa bed is a mainstay in many a first apartment, library, family room, and/or guest room. A sofa bed must be sized up even more carefully than a standard sofa, though, because of the mechanism that supports the fold-out mattress. You should check that the sofa bed opens and closes with ease, and without tearing the sheets; does a warranty cover the workings of the mechanism?

Check, too, that the mattress is thick and firm enough to lie on comfortably, both at the edge of the bed and in the middle. You do not want to feel a sag. Last but not least, you want to be sure that the sofa bed is capacious enough to accommodate two people if it is advertised as such.

Because a sofa bed is deeper, to accommodate the mechanism and mattress, you must measure the one you like accurately to be sure it will fit through doorways and around tight corners. Also, note how much room the sofa bed takes up when it is open; you want to be able to walk around it without feeling confined.

A sofa bed is very heavy, so you should know exactly where it will be installed so that you won't have to move it once it is set in place.

Sectional Sofa

A sectional sofa is simply that—a sofa too large to stand on its own, so it is divided into sections. These sections may be ordered separately and fitted together to conform to the configuration that will look best in your room. Or, because they are upholstered or finished on all sides, they may stand independently. Sectionals, in a word, are the most flexible of seating arrangements. A sectional sofa works particularly well in a large room where you want to create and set off a seating island.

The simplest sectional comprises one or two arm pieces (a left and/or a right), armless units, and units that turn the corner. The arm units may be elongated into one-armed chaises. Armless and backless end pieces may pull away from their mates to serve as ottomans.

Some sectionals come with compatible, low tables which substitute for corner units.

Working off your floor plan, add up the widths along the backs of the various segments you want to cluster together. How many units can you fit in your room? What shape do you want the sectional to assume? An L? An arc? A U? Do you want all the segments to abut, or would you like one or two sections to stand alone, to move about as needed?

Day Bed

A day bed is usually narrow, narrower than a twin bed. If it has a back, this will not be upholstered. The arms and the base both may be upholstered and boast a thick, mattresslike cushion. Day beds are usually softened with the addition of bolsters and/or pillows.

Futon

A popular and inexpensive alternative to a sofa is the futon, a folding, firm, tufted mattress covered in cotton that can rest directly upon the floor or be supported in its own wooden, convertible frame.

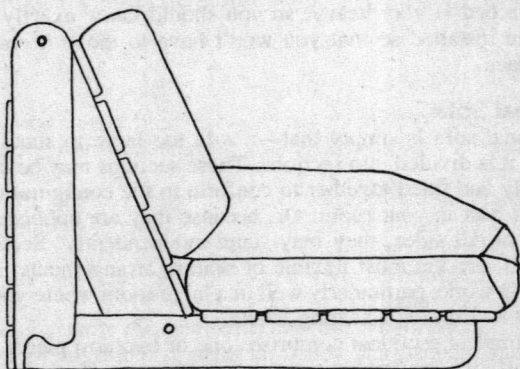

Folding Futon

Because the futon is usually selected as a crossover piece of furniture, the size you need will be dictated by whether or not it will be used as a bed, too.

Chaise Longue

A chaise looks like an elongated easy chair. It may have one arm or two arms; these are positioned lower than the back, which may be straight or curved, channeled or tufted, or left plain.

Ottoman

Cousin to the **footstool,** which is a low footrest that is usually upholstered only on top, the ottoman is often designed as a mate to an armchair. On its own, it may be square, rectangular, or rounded in silhouette. With a firm cushion or topped by a tray, a large ottoman may stand in for a coffee table. A truly adaptable ottoman will roll around on casters. An overscaled, round (and often tufted) ottoman may be called a *pouf*.

Once you have decided on your various pieces of upholstered furniture and where you would like to place them, it is time to think about the other pieces that will flesh out your overall furniture arrangement and decorating scheme. In the next chapter we will look at these pieces, which include smaller side chairs (that are not upholstered), tables, desks, storage units, and other less functional pieces that may serve no purpose other than to hold a plant or other object. We will talk about beds in the chapter that follows.

To Recap

- Upholstered furnishings—sofa, love seat, easy chairs—are the ones that—besides beds—are designed for sitting or lounging comfort.
- Buy the best-quality upholstered furniture you can afford.
- Check the construction of the piece—its frame, webbing, and springs—to be sure it is well-made.
- Before deciding on your fabric, look to see how the floor sample is covered.
- Check the cushions, too, because they are what you sit on and lean against, and you want them to feel right.
- Last but not least, be sure the piece you like will fit through the door, and that it will fit in its appointed spot in the room.

CHAPTER 9

Furniture

With upholstered furniture selected to establish comfort zones in your house, other pieces of furniture then can be fitted in to complete the decorating scheme. Side chairs, tables, and storage pieces such as dressers and bookcases flesh out each room in response to your individual needs and personal taste.

Most of these pieces will probably be made out of wood, or a woodlike substitute sheathed in another material such as plastic laminate. Other materials include stainless steel, wrought iron and other metals, glass (usually combined with metal), plastic, and wicker or rattan.

When Is Wood Wood?

Historically, a piece of wood furniture was, indeed, constructed of wood. These days that is often not the case. Many furniture manufacturers create their pieces from plywood, which are then sheathed in wood veneers (thin layers of wood that measure between $\frac{1}{16}''$ and $\frac{1}{32}''$ thick) because plywood, which comprises many layers of wood pressed and glued together (or composites such as particleboard, which is made from wood chips crushed, pressed, and glued together), are warp-free and often are far stronger than many woods.

Many antiques were also veneered. Beautiful veneer—usually of exotic or rare woods—had to be meticulously cut and pieced; a veneered antique can be extremely costly because of the workmanship involved in its manufacture.

Solid Wood
The term *solid wood* may be used for a piece of furniture that marries several materials. The term applies only to the exposed, or decorative, surfaces; the parts of the piece you do not see may be made of plywood or of another material altogether.

Advantages of Married Woods
Marrying solid woods, composites, and veneers may appear to be a cost-cutting measure, and so it is, in some cases. With the price of woods escalating all the time, though, and with some woods becoming either rare or virtually extinct, veneers can offer the appearance of an exotic or favored wood at a fraction of the cost.

Look closely at the craftsmanship of the veneer; do the little pieces that compose the veneer lie flat? Are their seams smooth? These features indicate high-quality workmanship.

Simulated Wood
Simulated wood is a plastic or paper laminate that assumes the appearance of wood and stands in for a wood veneer. Many inexpensive bookcases and other storage pieces that are promoted as having a wood finish are actually sheathed in a layer of simulated wood.

Hardwood versus Soft?
Most better-quality furniture is made of hardwood, such as oak; less expensive pieces may be made of a softwood, such as pine. Furniture may also be crafted of fruitwood, wood that, as the term implies, comes from fruit-bearing trees, such as apple.

Some traditionally preferred woods such as mahogany and walnut are becoming increasingly rare; their appearance may be rep-

licated by a stain finish over another hardwood instead. Check to
see if the piece you like is made of the actual wood, or, instead,
if only the veneer or the finish is of the wood proclaimed on the
label.

A Finished or Unfinished Back

Historically, many pieces of furniture such as chests of drawers
and highboys that were designed **not** to be seen on all sides were
crafted with backs (and drawer bottoms) of a lesser-grade, less
costly wood that was not polished or finished in any way. Thus,
a piece typically used for storage and display that is usually pushed
up against a wall will probably have a back made of a less substantial, thinner material.

If you plan on positioning a storage piece such as a blanket
chest in a room so that it will be visible on all four sides, you
should be sure to inspect it to see if it has a finished back made
to match or complement the front—or request that the piece be
custom-altered, if possible.

Green Wood

These days, too, some of the woods that are sawn and milled for
use in construction and cabinetry are not dried or aired out long
enough. When wood is used green, it is vulnerable to warping,
splitting, and splintering. Inexpensive furnishings (notably chairs
and tables) may be made of green wood. You should thoroughly
inspect every piece of furniture before you make your purchase;
look for any cracks and splinters in the frame, and especially
underneath the seat or base of the piece. Look, too, at the color
of the wood; it may, indeed, appear to have a greenish tinge.

Joints

When considering a piece of furniture for purchase, you should
always look at every point where pieces of wood are joined. If
two pieces of wood are simply pressed and glued or nailed together
end to end in what is known as a butt joint, they will probably
come apart with use and wear. A mitred joint, one in which the
two pieces have been cut at forty-five-degree angles before joining,
is not much stronger.

The strongest joints are those that are either dovetailed or formed
by a mortise and tenon, because these can lock together. Dovetails

Doweled Joint   **Buttressed Joint**

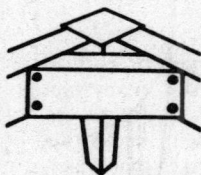

are little angled extrusions that fit, jigsawlike, into similarly formed cutouts in the adjoining pieces. In a mortise and tenon configuration, the extrusion, cut in on all sides, slides into a hole or cavity bored through the adjoining piece.

All joints should be glued, no matter how they fit together. Joints that must be extra strong—especially under chair seats and tabletops—are usually supplemented by corner braces, blocks of wood that are cut to fit and lock into place for extra stability. (On heavy, upholstered furnishings, corner blocks may be screwed as well as glued into position.)

Checking for Stability

Before you purchase a table or chair, it is a good idea to push it to check that it is balanced, that it stands sturdily upon its legs, and that it does not wobble or creak. If legs are thin, they should be strengthened and stabilized by stretcher rails, which are long pieces of wood used to connect them. Stretchers are usually linked in an H formation—paired front to back with another connecting them across the middle from rail to rail.

Stable Tables

A tabletop should fit securely to its legs, usually with an apron— a horizontal support—between. If the table comes with leaves, the sliding mechanism to accommodate them should open and close smoothly, and the leaves should fit snugly together, with no spatial interruption between them and the tabletop.

The same premise applies to drop leaves. These should flip up smoothly to rest upon pull-out supports with no visible droop or

Drop Leaf Table

sag. When they drop back down, they should hang straight, at a perpendicular angle to the tabletop. The supports should fold tidily in place.

A Comfortable Dining Table

Most tables—be they for dining or used for work or hobbies—are made to be 29″ or 30″ high, because this is the height that is comfortable for resting wrists or elbows upon the surface. The apron, which is the band of wood that drops down underneath the top of the table, cannot be too wide or it will inhibit crossing your legs while seated at the table. For dining, each person needs a minimum of 24″ width for elbow room. A table that is twice as long as it is wide is genially proportioned: 30″ × 60″ is commodious for six diners; 36″ × 72″ is comfortable for eight. (A longer table, though, should not exceed a 3′ width or it will appear gargantuan, unless it can be accommodated in a huge room.)

Inspecting Storage Pieces

Storage pieces, which the furniture industry classifies under the heading case goods, must be inspected even more thoroughly because of the complexity of construction. Here joinery makes a significant impact on strength and durability.

Construction of a Drawer

Each drawer in a dresser, chest, desk, or other storage unit should fit snugly within the frame of the overall piece. All stacked drawers should align, top and bottom and side to side. Each drawer should be guided and supported by a pair of smooth glides on either side, as well as by a center glide if the drawer is wide. Each drawer should be fitted with an automatic stop, too, so that it will not pull out all the way, unless you purposely lift it free of the frame. Best-quality drawers will be dovetailed at the corners, too.

The back and side panels of every drawer should measure at least ½" thick, for stability; the bottom may be made of a thinner panel, but it should also feel rigid to the touch. The entire drawer should be sanded and sealed (to rid it of splinters); it does not need to be polished or buffed, but it should be stained or otherwise finished to complement or match the face of the drawer in color and tone.

The hardware used to pull open each element—the knob on the door and the so-called pull on the drawer—should be even and straight. For a secure fit, each piece of hardware should be bolted from the inside.

How a Door Should Fit

Like drawers, doors should fit snugly within or close tightly upon the frame of a storage piece. A pair of doors should butt exactly, and align top and bottom. Tilting or off-kilter doors indicate haphazard assembly. Each door should open and close smoothly on its hinges; hinges on one door should line up with their mates on an adjacent door. Hinges should be strong and attached securely and should not wobble when the door is opened and shut. Best-quality hinges are bolted on the inside in the same manner as drawer pulls or doorknobs.

Shelves

Storage pieces, and especially bookcases, may be—and often are—strengthened and bolstered by one or more stationary shelves which are firmly affixed to the frame of the piece. For flexibility, though, most pieces include adjustable shelves. These usually rest upon tabs which lock or screw into predrilled holes. You can raise or lower the shelves to accommodate books or other objects by shifting the position of the tabs.

Ready-to-assemble bookcases are sold as kits, complete with a specified number of shelves and companion tabs. Depending upon the design, the bookcase may or may not come with a back and a base. R-T-A (ready to assemble) bookcases are typically fabricated of a core veneered with a laminated paper. The veneer may be colored white or black or simulate wood.

Unfinished bookcases can be bought in a variety of heights and widths. Widths usually increase in three-inch increments from 9″ to 48″. You can choose one of two depths: usually 9″ or 11¾″. You can also request that an unfinished bookcase be primed for painting.

Decorative Hardware

As mentioned previously, hardware should be sturdy. Ask if brass hardware is lacquered. Many manufacturers will coat brass plate with a protective lacquer to relieve the consumer of the hassle of polishing. If you inadvertently remove the lacquer with cleanser, you may remove the ''brass'' as well. Lacquered brass plate needs only to be dusted.

Antiques

These days, the term antique has broadened to apply to furniture that is over 50 rather than 100 years old; even pieces from the 1950s are being classified as antiques.

Why Buy Antiques?

Many antiques are cherished heirlooms that are passed down from one generation to another within a family. Other antiques, of course, may eventually be sold because succeeding generations may find these objects old-fashioned and they do not like them.

For the consumer, antiques are available at estate sales, at auctions, in antique shops, and in specialized departments in department stores. Antiques also show up at flea markets.

Obviously, there is no rule about buying antiques. Some people simply prefer the look or patina of the old; others are avid collectors of furnishings and decorative objects of a certain period. Antiques embody a sense of history. They speak to us of another era and of another lifestyle.

An antique, too, may simply catch our eye, and look and feel right. Whatever the reason, antiques continue to be sought after, not only by collectors, but also by people who like old things.

Reproductions

Antiques have always been and continue to be copied; line-for-line copies are called reproductions, and, if meticulously crafted of fine materials, they can be almost as valuable as the originals they emulate. Fine reproductions may be replicated from honored pieces in a museum collection or from a stately home in England, for example, or another trustworthy source such as a well-regarded private collection. Every effort is made to render the reproduction as perfect in every detail as possible. Such a reproduction can be costly, but is worth the investment.

Adaptations

Many furniture companies will "interpret" an antique. Instead of reproducing it precisely, they transform the design into a slightly altered variation of the original. Adaptations are made for two reasons: economy and comfort. Line-for-line copies can be extremely expensive to reproduce, especially if they require rare woods and other hard-to-find materials.

In terms of comfort, an adaptation—of a colonial wing chair, for example—might be more thickly upholstered than its original counterpart, or it might have a seat cushion where none existed before, or the same chair might be scaled down slightly or rounded in silhouette, or it may be slipcovered, or made of a wood that is simply stained and polished to emulate a more expensive, virtually extinct wood. There are any number of variations on a theme, and usually the variations are less costly than reproductions.

Occasional Furniture

The smaller pieces of furniture that basically fill in the gaps are called occasional or accent pieces. Occasional tables, for example, may include end tables, small card or backgammon tables, nesting tables, or tea tables.

Almost any small, portable piece falls in the category of accent furniture. Magazine racks, triple-tiered stands (some are called muffin stands), footstools, candlestands, hat racks, vitrines (which are tabletop or wall-hung, glassed-in display cases), standing mirrors, such as the cheval—the list goes on and on.

Occasional and accent pieces may exhibit contemporary styling, or they may be antiques, reproductions, or adaptations. Some manufacturers craft occasional and accent pieces to be assembled at home; these can be purchased both retail or by mail order.

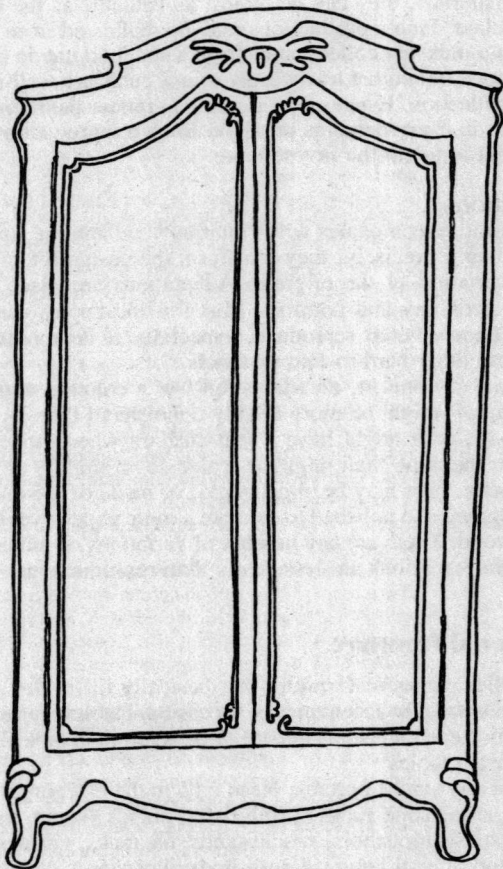

Armoire

SOME SPECIAL PIECES TO CONSIDER FOR YOUR HOME

Armoire
French for wardrobe. Because it is a massive piece, it's usually crafted to be disassembled when moved. Has single or double doors, often carved. May have drawer beneath, or shelves and/or pole inside.

Blanket chest
Deep boxlike chest with hinged lid. So called because it often stands at the bottom of a bed, for linen storage. Often painted.

Breakfront
Alternate term for **china, china cupboard,** or **dresser,** when the latter refers to china storage. So called because of its projecting center section. Glass-paned doors above, drawers and/or solid doors below.

Buffet
Alternate term for **sideboard.** Waist-high cupboard; top used for serving foods. Drawers store linens and flatware.

Bureau
Term may apply to a long, low **chest of drawers** used in a bedroom, or to a **writing desk.**

Butler's table
Most common version comprises two sections: an oval tray with hinged leaves, two of which have slots for lifting; and a base. The base may be stationary, or it may fold.

Campaign chest
Small, low, flat-bottomed chest of drawers embellished with metal corner brackets and squared metal pulls set into rectangular escutcheons. Variation: **campaign bed,** with mattress resting upon drawers.

China
Casual term for china cupboard.

Console table
Small table affixed to wall and supported only on front legs. One variation is the demilune, so called because of its half-moon shaped top.

Credenza
Long, low storage cabinet. Often used in offices. May be used as a **buffet**.

Dresser
A multipurpose term, often used as an alternative to **china,** especially when the china cupboard has an upper section that is set back, like a **hutch,** with open shelves for display. The term may also be used as an alternative to **chest of drawers,** especially if a mirror is placed above it.

Entertainment center
Another term for a wall system that accommodates electronic gear such as a television, VCR, and stereo.

Étagère
Tall, narrow, multitiered, usually open, freestanding shelf system. Narrow corner supports. Often made of metal with glass or mirrored shelves.

Highboy
Tall chest on stand. Stand, which usually matches a lowboy, also has drawers. Top drawers of chest often paired and shallower than lower drawers. Antique highboys could be elaborately detailed.

Huntboard/Sideboard

Huntboard	Originated in the South as a taller, narrower version of the **sideboard.**
Hutch	An alternate term for **dresser.** A two-part china cupboard, with open shelves above and a stand, on legs, with drawers below.
Lingerie chest	Tall, narrow chest of drawers. Also called a **semanier** because each of its seven drawers was reserved for one day of the week.
Lowboy	Low chest of drawers on legs. Usually a shallow center drawer, flanked by paired, deeper drawers. Often designed to be compatible with or to match a highboy.
Plate rack	A multitiered open shelf, used to showcase dishes. May have hooks for hanging cups or mugs. Often suspended above a sideboard.
R-T-A Furniture	Ready-to-assemble furniture, formerly known as **K-D,** or knock-down, furniture. Packaged in kit form with instructions and hardware, and often with basic tools.
Secretary	Slant-topped desk with drawers beneath writing surface. May come in two sections. Tall, shallow storage case above the writing surface may have solid or glass-paned doors.

Wall system   A tall, modular storage system comprising multiple open
and closed units (some may have glass panes). Called a
wall system because it is so big it virtually fills a wall.
Often used to house an **entertainment system,** books,
CDs, and tapes. May also house a bar and a desk. May
include corner pieces to link units. Units may also be
linked by a high bridge, especially if the connection is
being made over a bed or over an integrated buffet. May
be lit within for showcasing displays.

Because of their size, occasional and accent pieces fit in almost
anywhere you desire. Like accessories, they are hallmarks of individual taste. A bed, though, offers separate challenges, and
decisions. The following chapter will tell you what to look for in
a bed and its mattress, pillows, linens, and dressings.

To Recap

- Furniture should be constructed to last.
- Check every single separate part of a piece of furniture, and
  then check how sturdily and smoothly the pieces fit together.
- If wood, check the composition of the piece; if wood veneer,
  be sure the veneer adheres well.
- Reproductions and adaptations are made to bring antique
  styles into an affordable price range and to ensure contemporary comfort, too.
- Occasional and accent pieces fill in the gaps in a decorating
  scheme.

CHAPTER 10

Beds and Bedding

Because of wear and tear, few antique beds survived into the twentieth century. People today, too, tend to be taller and heavier than their ancestors; most old beds you find will have to be retrofitted for comfort.

The simplest solution for sleeping is a mattress on the floor or a futon. The next step up is to assemble a Harvard frame, a two-part metal frame on casters that supports a box spring and mattress. Harvard frames expand; the slimmest accommodates both a twin and a double mattress. To gussy up such a bed, you can add a headboard and a footboard.

Bed Styles

Beds today come in a wide variety of styles, from formal four-posters and canopy beds to child-friendly campaign beds with

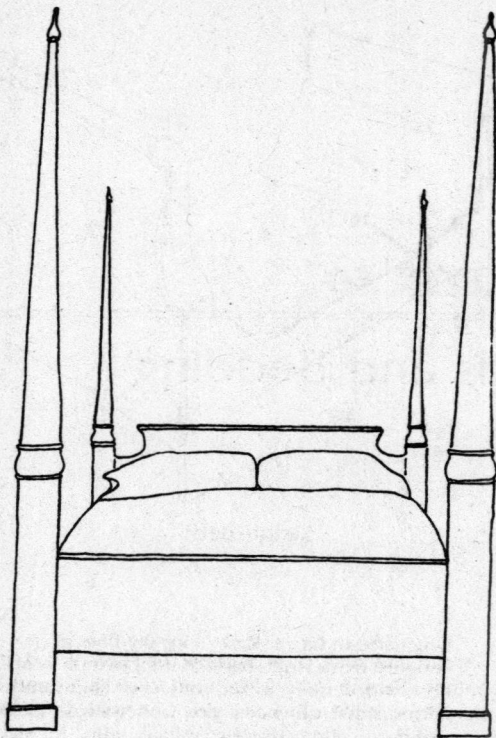

Four-Poster Bed

storage drawers beneath. You can select a bed to be compatible with a particular decorating style or simply for comfort.

Campaign bed	Boxlike base supports mattress. Two or three drawers on a side or tiers of drawers (to raise the bed higher) embellished with recessed decorative pulls. Usually stained, painted, or covered with plastic laminate.
Four-poster	Term used for a bed with posts at the four corners. May support a canopy and/or bed hangings.

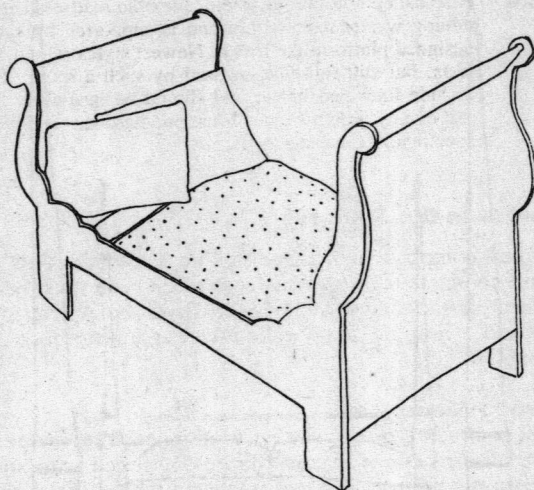

Sleigh Bed

Futon	Originated in Japan. Rests upon the floor or on a specially designed frame; folds back on itself to form a sofa. Usually filled with densely packed cotton padding, sometimes with polyester fiberfill or feathers. Upholstered in a thick, natural-hued cotton covering, usually tufted for stability.
Murphy bed	Bed, usually framed and supported by a wall system, that swings down for sleeping, flips back up into its own "closet" when not in use.
Platform bed	Mattress rests on a raised inverted box. Platform may be stained or painted, or covered in the same wall-to-wall carpeting as the floor.
Sleigh bed	Resembles a sleigh because it has a high, scrolled headboard and footboard. Twin bed size is often placed sideways against the wall, like a daybed.
Tester bed	A Southern term for a canopy bed. A variation is the half-tester, with its partial canopy cantilevering over the head of the bed.
Trundle bed	A low, narrow bed on casters or wheels, which rolls under a larger bed when not in use.

Water bed   Also called a flotation system. Flexible mattress/bag (containing water) rests within and is supported by specially designed platformlike frame. Newest styles mimic "real" beds, but still must be encased by such a frame. Should include liner and heater and should be insulated. Should rest evenly within frame. Must purchase sheets developed specifically for water beds.

Comfort Is in the Mattress

A good bed comprises more than just an assembly of its parts. To ensure complete comfort while you sleep, you must be especially attentive to what you choose to sleep on. A poor-quality mattress and a limp or lumpy pillow can aggravate back and/or neck trouble.

Innerspring Mattresses

The most common type of mattress is an innerspring mattress, so called because its frame encases dozens of coiled wire springs. An innerspring mattress is usually teamed with a matching box spring, a stiff-framed foundation that also contains supportive springs.

Checking a Box Spring

The sturdiest mattress/box spring sets have frames made of wood. A box spring's coils are attached securely to a slatted base, which is generally protected by a taut muslin cover. The rest of the box spring is covered in the same fabric as its companion mattress. One hallmark of quality is the thickness of the cover; it may also be quilted, at least on the sides, and seams should be even and smooth, with no puckers. All four corners of the box spring should be sheathed with plastic protectors, to keep the fabric from wearing out.

Construction of an Innerspring Mattress

The individual coils within an innerspring frame may or may not be individually encased, but they should be individually tied both to the frame and to each other. The mattress should feel as stable at the edges as it does at the middle; there should be no sag. You should not feel the coils at all. The best-quality mattresses are thickly padded. The fabric cover should be thick and taut and the seams even. A mattress cover will also be quilted, and the quilting should not pucker. Check that the mattress has at least four ventilation holes on the sides; the holes allow air to circulate through the mattress. This prevents the mattress from developing an odor from body oils. Finally, there should be handles on the sides so that you can flip the mattress when desired.

Testing an Innerspring Mattress

The construction of the innerspring mattress is of paramount importance to your sleeping comfort. Mattresses are categorized by their firmness. Generally, the heavier you are, the firmer your mattress should be. A mattress that is too soft will exacerbate a back problem, too.

Before you make your purchase, lie down on a number of mattresses to ascertain which feels the best to you. If you will be sharing your bed, both partners should test the mattress.

One way to test a mattress is to lie on your back, placing your hand between the small of your back and the mattress; you should be able to feel both sides of your hand, with a little give. Then, roll onto your side. How does the mattress feel at your head, neck, shoulders, hips, and knees?

If you will be sharing your mattress, both of you should lie down side by side. Fold your hands under your heads; do you have enough elbow room?

MATTRESS SIZES

Twin (and long twin)	39″ × 75″ or 80″ or 84″
Full (or double, and long double)	54″ × 75″ or 80″ or 84″
Queen	60″ × 80″
King	76″ × 80″
California (or Hollywood)	72″ × 84″

Maintaining an Innerspring Mattress

If you decide to buy an innerspring mattress, you should turn it around every week or so, and flip it every month, for the first six months, if not longer. Your mattress has to settle and become accustomed to your weight. It is a good idea to air your mattress every time you change the sheets, to release any moisture built up from the heat of your body during sleep. (Airing the mattress simply means leaving it alone for a couple of hours before replacing the sheets.)

Foam Mattresses

A foam mattress, made of fairly dense polyurethane foam (which may or may not have one side molded to form a bumpy "egg crate" surface) is generally used alone, without a foundation. A foam mattress is usually selected for a frameless bed such as a platform bed, a Murphy bed, or bunk beds. An easy-to-fold foam mattress may also be chosen as a replacement mattress for a sofa bed. One advantage of foam mattresses is that they are nonallergenic. They are also lightweight and inexpensive. Foam, though, may crumble over time, and it may begin to emit an unpleasant odor as it decomposes.

Mattress Pads

A quilted mattress pad will also help absorb moisture, and it adds a layer of softness between the satiny mattress and bottom sheet. A mattress pad may be completely fitted, like a fitted sheet, or it may lie on top of the mattress and be anchored by corner elastics. The pad stabilizes the bottom sheet, helps keep it from wrinkling and shifting during the night, and allows it to breathe. The pad also keeps the mattress clean by inhibiting transmission of skin oils.

Pillows

For comfort, you should take special care to select a pillow of the correct firmness for you. Pillows are labeled accordingly: soft, medium, firm, or extra firm. For those who suffer from neck pain, therapeutic pillows are also available; many designs incorporate a raised section, like a roll, to cradle the neck.

Your choice of firmness may depend upon the position you assume during sleep. If you spend most of the night on your side, you may prefer a firmer pillow than if you lie on your back or stomach. Those who sleep on their stomachs usually prefer a softer pillow.

Pillow Sizes

A pair of standard pillows, which measure 20″ × 26″ each, will fit, side by side, on a full-size (or double) bed. If you opt for a queen-size bed, you may want to purchase a pair of queen-size pillows to fit; these are four inches longer than the standard. King-size pillows are ten inches longer than the standard.

PILLOWCASE SIZES

Standard	20″ × 26″	
Queen	20″ × 34″	
King	20″ × 40″	

Accessory Pillows

In addition, you may want to add an accessory pillow or two to your pillow lineup. A breakfast pillow, which is a miniature version of a standard pillow, measures 10″ × 15″; a neck roll is the same length, and is usually about 6″ thick. A European square, so called because it is commonly used abroad, is a robust 26″ square. Because of their size, European squares are usually removed for sleeping. Europeans also often run a long bolster, which looks like an extended neck roll, along the headboard, partially for looks and partially to provide additional support behind other pillows while reading in bed.

Pillow Fills

A pillow's firmness may be dictated by the filling material. The softest pillows are filled with goose down or with a down and feather combination. People with allergies may want to avoid down, however. Another disadvantage to down is that pillows filled with this material cannot be washed.

Resilient polyester fiberfill can be washed and is nonallergenic. Polyester fiberfill is not as soft as down, but it is available in a variety of firmnesses.

The firmest material is foam. Foam is also very springy. Over time, foam may crumble and emit an unpleasant odor, though.

Pillow Protectors

Even though pillows come encased in fabric, it is a good idea to protect them with zip-on cotton covers because of the transmission of hair oils, which will stain them over time. These covers can be removed and washed, and replaced when necessary, to enhance the life of the pillow.

Comforters

Like pillows, comforters may be filled with down, with down and feathers, or with polyester fiberfill. Many polyester-filled comforters are designed to be part of a bedding ensemble; many down and down-and-feather comforters, on the other hand, are meant to be encased in a duvet, a French term for a pillowcaselike comforter cover. Because down comforters cannot be washed as poly-filled comforters can, a washable duvet is a boon.

COMFORTER SIZES

Twin	66″ × 86″
Full	78″ or 81″ × 86″
Queen	86″ or 88″ × 92″
King	102″ or 107″ × 92″

Bedspreads and Dust Ruffles

Many sheet manufacturers offer the option of bedcovers: comforter or bedspread. A bedspread may fall to the floor on three sides, or it may be shortened to reveal a companion dust ruffle or bed skirt.

The length of a standard dust ruffle is 17″, which is the height of a standard Harvard frame plus the width of a box spring. A dust ruffle is softly gathered; a bed skirt is more strictly tailored, usually with box pleats at the corners.

BEDSPREAD SIZES

Twin	81″ × 110″
Full	96″ × 110″
Queen	102″ × 110″
King	120″ × 118″

Bed Linens

One of the ways you can explicitly personalize your bedrooms and alter their mood is with bedding. If you purchase two or three sets of sheets and cases, you can completely change a bedroom's decor.

Bedding manufacturers have taken the hassle out of tying in bed linens with window treatments. These days you can purchase coordinated ensembles that may include flat and fitted sheets and pillowcases, as well as pillow shams (these are trimmed on four sides and are accessed from the back), comforters and/or bedspreads, bed skirts or dust ruffles, accessory pillows, window valances and curtains, and even table rounds and shower curtains.

One easy way to change the look of a bedroom is to buy compatible solid-colored sheets and cases or shams, and mix and match solids with patterns whenever you change your bed.

Thread Count

Finest-quality sheets have a very high thread count (as much as 200 to 250 threads to the inch, or more), and are all cotton. These days, most quality all-cotton sheets are treated so that they need not be ironed. Otherwise, no-iron sheets are woven in a 50/50 (or other proportion) blend with polyester.

Least-costly blended sheets, with a 120- or 180-thread count, are called muslin sheets. These feel coarser than their all-cotton counterparts.

Flannel Sheets

For winter warmth, flannel sheets are an option. These are typically made of cotton and have a soft feel or hand. They come in an increasingly fashionable range of colors and patterns.

UNFITTED BED SHEET SIZES

Twin	66″ × 96″
Full	81″ × 96″
Queen	90″ × 102″
King	108″ × 102″

Blankets

With the advent of comforters, blankets began to be used less frequently, except as accents. Several types of blanket can be considered: thermal blankets—usually cotton, but sometimes wool—display an open weave or waffle weave, which allows for air flow to help release moisture from your body, so you don't feel sweaty. Cotton thermals are washable; wool thermals must be dry cleaned.

Wool blankets are quite expensive; the most woollike synthetic, acrylic, is an economical alternative, and can be washed. Acrylic, unlike wool, resists moths.

Electric blankets, made of acrylic, are a good solution for those who prefer to keep the thermostat low during the winter.

BLANKET SIZES

Twin	66″ × 96″
Full	80″ × 96″
Queen	90″ × 96″
King	108″ × 96″

To a bedding lineup, you may want to add a wool or cotton throw (really, just a small blanket) or quilt for extra coziness in case of a breeze or chill.

Amplifying Comfort

With furniture in place and tactile comfort zones established, it is time to consider other aspects of your decorating scheme that make you feel at home: windows and lighting.

To Recap

- Beds come in a wide range of styles but, because you spend so much time in bed, it is best to make comfort your first priority; comfort is dictated, first and most importantly, by the mattress and box spring you choose.
- A mattress will last for years; test mattresses in the store, and then invest in the best you can afford.
- An innerspring mattress is paired with a box spring; a foam mattress can be used alone.
- Invest in best-quality pillows, too. Buy these in the firmness that feels right to you.
- Bed linens, blankets, comforters, and dust ruffles all contribute to a room's decor; mix and/or match to create a look you will love.
- You can change the look of your bedroom with a change of bedding; experiment!

CHAPTER 11

Window Dressings

From our windows, we gaze upon our surroundings; in turn, people outside may gaze upon us. Windows, therefore, are usually screened, at least transparently, with some sort of covering, to ensure a sense of privacy. Windows are covered, too, to subdue strong doses of daylight and inhibit glare. A covering may also help insulate a room when it is cold outside, close out an ugly view, or camouflage an awkwardly shaped window.

The Standard Window

A standard window comprises a number of elements: a frame or casing (including trim), sashes (the glass-filled, or glazed, panels), sill, and apron (the portion of the enclosure that drops below the sill). Most windows are double-hung; that is, they have two sashes that overlap and lock at the center of the window where they meet.

Each sash may enclose a single pane, or the sashes may contain a number of smaller panes that are separated by wood, plastic, or metal strips called muntins. Multipane windows are defined by the number of panes per sash; a six-over-six, for example, describes a window with six panes within each sash.

Historically, windows were made of wood. The best-quality windows are still made of wood; the best of these, too, are most likely to be crafted so that even thermal windows have "divided lights"; their individual panes are enclosed within muntins. Other window materials include aluminum and vinyl-clad aluminum.

Other Window Types

Windows are one indicator of the style of a house. Many houses built during the Victorian era, for example, boast bay windows, three-sided windows that protrude from the facade. Many ranch houses feature sliding glass doors and picture windows. Postmodern houses, built during the 1980s, affected the Palladian window, a standard window capped with an arched half-moon window, or lunette.

Thermal Windows

These days, when windows are expected to insulate as well as afford a view, many are designed as thermals. Thermal windows comprise two layers of glass that sandwich a layer of air or gas that repels outside cold and heat. Most thermal windows are not divided into panes; to effect a multipaned look, window manufacturers provide muntin grids which are snapped into place on the inside of the window. (Snap-in grids are convenient because they can be snapped out when the window needs to be washed.)

A Role in Decoration

Window coverings, or window treatments as they are known in the trade, play a role in decoration. That role may be peripheral, especially if the need for privacy is minimal. Or windows may assume a greater presence in a decorating scheme; some treatments, indeed, can be as elaborate, or more elaborate, than any other element in a room.

A Carefree Component

These days, with the trend in decorating toward a more natural, personal, informal, and eclectic mood, windows are being treated in a more casual manner.

Many manufacturers, especially of bed linens, have created prepackaged window coverings as essential coordinates to their patterns. These packages usually team a valance with a pair of curtains; a soft shade may also be added to the mix. The added bonus of these packages is that they eliminate the hassle of complicated installation. The manufacturer's instructions are easy to follow, too. They always suggest the hardware that is needed for each layer and then tell you step-by-step how to go about hanging each for the prettiest effect.

Soft versus Hard

Window coverings are classified in two ways: soft and hard. Because they are made of fabric, curtains and draperies, for instance, are considered to be soft; hard treatments include aluminum miniblinds, wooden venetian blinds, and shutters.

Measuring a Window

You must take accurate measurements of each window before buying and installing any window treatment. If you are installing a shade or blind, most likely you will need to know only the height and width of the window casing.

If you want to hang curtains or draperies, you will have to take into account other measurements: the space between the ceiling and the top of the casing (so you can establish where you want to install the rod or pole), the extreme width of the window (from the outside edge of the casing on one side of the window across to the other) plus several inches on either side to allow room for installing brackets or other hardware, and the distance from the top of the casing and/or the hardware to the sill or to the floor.

If you are hanging café curtains, which cover only half the window, you will need to measure only the height and width of the lower sash, or bottom half of the window, to figure out the size you will need. If you hang two pairs of café curtains, one over the other, this is called a tiered effect. Another idea is to hang a short valance across the top of the window instead of an upper tier.

Curtain and Drapery Drop

Curtains are generally hung using the outside perimeter of the casing or trim as a guide. The decision you have to make regarding how far they should fall is up to you: do you want them to hang to and graze the sill, to cover the apron, or to fall all the way to the floor? Manufacturers recommend that curtains fall 4" below the sill, however, so that the hem is not visible from outside the window.

Curtains may hang to the floor, too. Draperies always hang to the floor. Both may simply graze the floor, or they may be allowed to fall or puddle right onto the floor for a truly luxurious effect. If you have wall-to-wall carpeting in the room, it is best to leave a one-inch gap so that the curtains or draperies may pull back easily.

Soft window coverings should be allowed to hang and fall naturally on either side of the window. They should also look good when they are closed. Draperies require a clearance of at least one foot to either side of the window casing to accommodate their hardware.

Curtains—especially lightweight, sill-length curtains—may hang within the window opening instead. Café curtains, which are tiered pairs of short, ruffled curtains, may hang inside or outside the casing.

Curtains

Curtains and draperies are differentiated both in their construction and in their installation. Curtains are lighter in weight and generally more billowy and informal in appearance; they are often unlined. In fact, curtains can appear quite transparent and gauzy.

Curtains are pulled back and away from the window manually, and, if you want them to stay out of the way, they must be tied back in some manner, either with a tieback, which is usually a little belt made of a matching or coordinating fabric (or it may be a tassel and cord), or with a piece of curtain hardware called a holdback. Holdbacks can be shaped like hooks or knobs; the curtain rests freely upon the holdback; it is not tied to it.

Curtains are usually hemmed at the top (this hem is called a header or a rod pocket) so that they can be gathered along a rod or pole or they are hemmed and suspended from curtain rings,

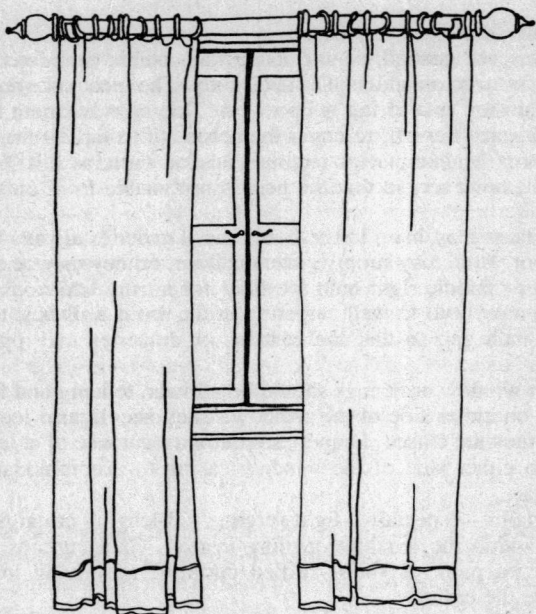

**Curtains on Rod and Rings
with Finials**

which, in turn, run along the pole. One specialty curtain is the tab curtain; tabs are fabric loops that run along a pole or rod in the place of rings.

Figuring Fullness

The main rule governing the fullness of a curtain is: the fuller the better. Fullness is governed by the gathers along the top or header of a curtain (or pleats for draperies). The more gathered the header, the fuller the curtain will be.

You should double—or even triple—the width of each of the two curtain panels. In other words, when flattened out, each panel should be at least as wide as the window opening itself—and even wider if the fabric is sheer or very lightweight.

Curtain Rods

Curtains are installed on wooden curtain poles, called decorator or dec rods, or on adjustable metal rods. The most common type of curtain rod is a spring tension rod. This type is spring loaded so that it can be compressed or lengthened to fit a window opening. The rod is held in place by rubber suction cups, and, of course, by the tension created by the spring mechanism.

An alternate type of straight metal curtain rod, also adjustable, rests in a pair of brackets that must be screwed into the window casing or wall. Another adjustable curtain rod curves at the ends; this type of rod is also supported by brackets. A thick, flat rod, used primarily to tightly gather a curtain for a tightly gathered, or shirred, effect, is the continental rod.

All of these rods are easy to install; simply screw the brackets in the wall and place the rod in the brackets. It is a good idea to double-check the manufacturer's instructions, though, in case there is a special hint or tip to help you out.

Rod Placement

Rods should be installed at least four inches above the window casing, so that the header and hardware will not show through the window. If your wall is embellished with a picture molding, which is a molding that runs around the wall to hang pictures from, consider tucking the rod underneath so that the top of the header runs flush with the underside of the molding.

Curtain Poles

Wooden decorator rods, which may be plain or fluted (incised with grooves), are packaged with a set of brackets and requisite screws and installation instructions. The package may also include rings. You screw the brackets in the wall and rest the rod upon them; the rings are an option if you want your curtains to be suspended from them rather than gathered along the rod.

If your window is exceptionally wide—like a plate glass window, for example—it is recommended that you support the pole with an extra, centrally positioned bracket that can be purchased separately. Otherwise, the weight of the curtain may make the pole buckle.

Curtain poles are typically embellished with finials, wooden decorative elements that screw directly into the ends of the pole. Finials assume myriad shapes; the two most common styles are a ball and an acorn.

Sew-Yourself Curtains

Curtains are surprisingly easy to make yourself. For a header, sew a casing—the hemlike tubular opening—across the top just wide enough to slide along the rod or pole of your choice; hem the sides and bottom; then gather the curtain on its rod or pole.

When you cut fabric for a curtain, figure on adding enough to the length of the fabric to make the casing for the rod or pole of your choice; this measurement will vary from 2" to 4", depending upon the diameter of the rod or pole. Then add another 3" or 4" for the bottom hem.

Another way to make a header is with prestrung gathering tape. This tape comes in a variety of widths. Thicker tape gives the appearance of shirring; thinner tape of simple gathering.

Making a Curtain

Once you take the measurements of your curtain panel into account, lay out the curtain fabric on a table or floor and cut it out accordingly. Leave the panel flat. Turn down the top of the panel ½" and iron it flat. Then lay the header tape across the adjusted top of your fabric and pin it in place with straight pins. Sew on the tape, following the marks indicated on the tape, by hand or on a sewing machine, to create the casing.

Then, pull the strings to the exact width you want and tie them off. Cut off excess string and slide the curtain on the rod.

Curtains from Sheets

An even easier method is to use sheets. Sheets are prehemmed and a twin sheet can stand in for one curtain without sewing a single stitch. Slit the narrower, bottom hem of the sheet to create a pocket and then slide the sheet onto the rod. If the sheet features a wide, embellished top hem (also called a turnback), this will look pretty grazing the windowsill or floor.

The only time you have to use the turnback itself as the header, rather than the bottom hem, is when the sheet pattern would look strange upside down. Look at your sheet closely to see which direction it should hang.

Draperies

Draperies, which tend to be more formal than curtains, are also more complicated in their fabrication. For one thing, they are usually lined with a complementary fabric that adds to their body. Because draperies are often made from more expensive fabrics, the liners also afford protection from the sun. Draperies are often interlined as well with a special stiffened intermediary fabric to further stabilize their construction. They may be insulated, too. Their bottom hems may be studded with weights to hold their folds in place.

Draperies may hang straight, in panels, over an extra set of sheer underdraperies, or they may pull back and forth across the window. In the latter case, they must be made wide enough to cover the windows. Some draperies assume specialty looks, such as the bishop's sleeve, in which the panels are caught and tied in tiered poufs.

Draperies, like curtains, should be full; fullness depends upon the type and spacing of pleats.

Pleats

Draperies are usually constructed with pleats along the header. The first, and most common type of pleat is a threefold pleat called a pinch pleat, or French pleat. The spacing between French pleats will vary depending upon the width of the window and the fullness of the fabric desired—the wider the window, the wider the spacing between the pleats. If the pleats are spaced too closely together, the fullness of the fabric may seem exaggerated.

A second and softer-looking type of pleat is the pencil or accordion pleat; these narrow pleats (as narrow as pencils, hence the name) run continuously across the heading. The last type is the box pleat; these evenly spaced pleats fold back upon themselves so that their creased edges align.

When calculating fabric for draperies, manufacturers use the term *pleated to*. This signifies the difference between the actual fabric width and the final, finished drapery width once the pleats are inserted.

Drapery Hardware

French pleated draperies hang from elongated three-pronged, S-shaped hooks called pin-on hooks that are pushed up along their headers. The hooks, or clips, are then hung through eyes, or miniature rings, that run along tracks (called slides or runners) set into drapery rods. These rods, which are usually adjustable, are

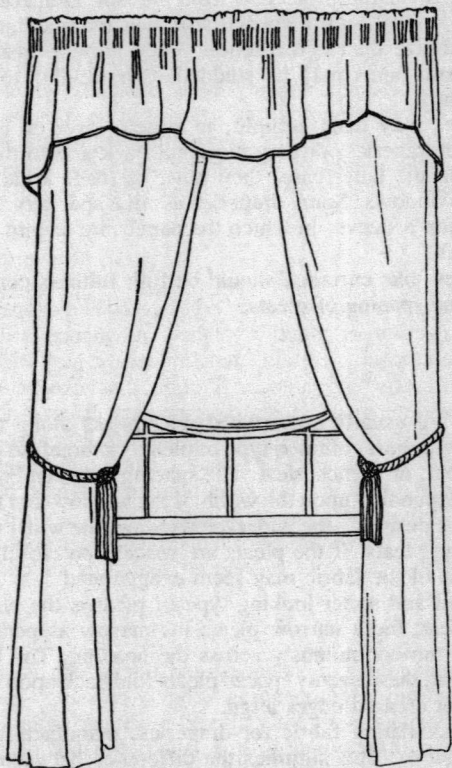

**Curtains with Valance
and Tassel Tiebacks**

called traverse rods. Traverse simply means that the rod crosses the window.

The traverse rod also accommodates a pulley and cord system that mechanically pulls the draperies back and out of the way. Because their construction is more complex, and the draperies they support are heavy, traverse rods, unlike thin, lightweight curtain rods, must be installed outside the window frame. If a window is wide, the rod must be supported by an additional grip, usually centered where draperies meet.

Drapery hardware is more complicated to install than curtain hardware because there are more pieces, but you can do it yourself. Follow the manufacturer's instructions. Basically, you screw supporting brackets into the wall (as you would for a curtain rod), as well as the pulley mechanism. The main thing to remember is to align the various pieces of the system correctly, especially if it comprises two or three separate traverse rods.

Valances

Both curtains and draperies can be highlighted and capped off with a crowning decoration called a valance. A valance is basically a shortened version of a curtain, and, indeed, it may match a pair of curtains exactly. A valance, though, can also be sewn and tailored to achieve a special, complementary effect.

A valance may run in gathers or pleats straight across the underlying window treatment, or it may assume one of several specialty contours. Of these, the most popular is the arch. Another is the cloud, comprising gentle poufs.

For added decorative interest, valances can be accentuated with rosettes or bows or knots formed of matching or coordinating fabric.

Swags

Another popular type of valance—and one which is often used alone, without any accompanying window dressing—is the swag or festoon. A swag is a gently curved piece of fabric tethered at the top corners of the window. It is usually finished off with soft, zigzag side panels of fabric called cascades, which hang down at either side. When a swag is rigorously constructed with rigid pleated sides, it is called a swag and jabot.

Swag and Jabots

Swags should be curved in a drop that is proportioned correctly for the width of the window. If the drop is too deep, it may look top heavy; conversely, it can look skimpy. Eyeball variations on the drop with a soft length of fabric until you find a drop that looks right to you.

Cornices

Draperies may also be accentuated with a cornice, a shallow, fabric-covered box that encloses and projects beyond the heading to hide the hardware. The fabric typically matches that of the hanging coverings, although it may be embellished separately.

The cornice may be absolutely rectangular, or it may be cut and shaped for added effect. The cornice may also be cut to hang

Cornice or Pelmet

down the sides of the casing, or it may have sides that continue to the floor. If a box completely surrounds the window, it is called a lambrequin.

The cornice is anchored to the wall with screws and stiff L-shaped metal brackets—usually a pair at either end. One of the pair is positioned at the top of the cornice and one at the bottom.

Roller Shades

There are a variety of ready-made window shades that are available at any home center or decorating outlet. The most familiar is the roller shade—or roller blind—which is simply a length of fabric (old-fashioned shades were deep green glazed canvas) that pulls down with a ring on a cord and rolls back up with a tug that releases a spring in the roller. Roller shades may roll in one of two ways: the conventional roll drops the fabric from the back of the roller (so the face of the shade is actually the inside of the shade); the reverse roll descends from the front of the roller.

A shade most commonly mounts within the window casing, about two inches from the top to allow for smooth operation. A pin in the wooden roller fits into one of two brackets that are installed inside the casing. When you purchase a shade, ask for the roller length that most closely approximates the width of your window—with ¼″ leeway for the pin to fit into the cap. To arrive at an exact fit, you may have to remove the metal cap and pin at one end of the roller and saw off the excess wood.

Replace the cap and pin, and install the shade using the hardware that is packaged with the shade.

If you want privacy without sacrificing light, ask for a bottom-up shade; this is identical to a standard roller shade, but it rolls up from the sill instead of down from the top of the window.

Cover Your Own Roller Shades
Plain roller shades may be laminated with fabric to match or coordinate with the decor using spray adhesive, which is available at craft shops or at your home center or decorator outlet.

First, unroll the shade and lay it flat; center the fabric of your choice on the shade and cut it to measure, leaving a ½″ overlap for trimming later. (Try to work with a piece of fabric that is wider than the shade as seams inhibit a smooth roll-up.) Then, spray adhesive evenly over the entire surface of the shade. Press the fabric over the sticky surface, working from top to bottom and from the center to the edges, smoothing out wrinkles and bubbles as you go. Trim excess and allow the adhesive to dry before rolling the shade back up.

Roller Shade Kits

Another way to create a roller shade is to work with the fabric of your choice and a roller shade kit. These kits, also available in home centers and decorator shops, prepackage an iron-on backing with a roller, narrow wooden slat, cord and ring, and all the necessary hardware.

The kit recommends that you avoid sheer, stretchy, or gauzy fabrics as these do not bond well with the backing provided.

Working on a large surface such as a big table or the floor, measure and cut the fabric to fit your window, adding a seam allowance of ½" on all sides. Lay out the backing and peel off its protective paper lining. Center and place the fabric on top of the backing. Iron with a dry iron at the setting recommended in the kit instructions. Iron from top to bottom, and from center to edges. Allow to cool completely, and then trim away the seam allowance on the sides.

With a do-it-yourself shade of this type, it looks best if you squeeze out a bead, or continuous trickle of white fabric or craft glue along the edges of the shade to prevent fraying. Rub or smear the glue into the edges; allow to dry.

Or you can bind the edges with a very thin tape or ribbon that will not inhibit the smooth roll-up of the shade. Tape or ribbon can be glued on with fabric glue.

Turn under the top of the shade and align it with the premarked line on the roller. Staple the shade to the roller, and assemble the roller and hardware as outlined in the kit instructions.

Fold under the bottom hem around slat; pin hem; leave ends open (to reinsert slat later). Sew hem; insert slat; sew ends closed. Center and attach the cord and ring.

Hemming a Shade

For added visual interest, you may want to cut a scalloped hem for your shade. First, consider how wide and deep you would like the scallops to be, and then, with a measuring tape, calculate how many scallops will fit along the bottom edge of the shade. Draw and cut a template of the scallops. Trace the scallops; cut. You can finish off the edge by sewing or gluing on binding along the edge.

Adding a Slat Over the Hem

Because a scalloped hem precludes insertion of a slat along the bottom of the shade, some people stabilize the shade by inserting the slat about 4½″ up from the hem. To do this, you have to sew a casing—which you can make from a strip of seam binding—along the back of the shade. (Make certain that the seam binding is wider than your slat so that it will slide in easily.) Position the strip of seam binding on the back of the shade; pin it in place. Sew. Insert the slat. Remove cord, if any, from the curtain ring and then center the ring over the slat on the front of the shade; sew on the ring.

Roman Shades

The Roman shade, which folds up accordionlike into stiff, wide horizontal pleats when it is raised, is a tailored window treatment that looks best when left alone, without accompanying window treatments, or capped with a plain cornice wrapped in a matching or coordinating fabric. Roman shades may be installed within or aligned with the outside edge of the window casing. The pleats are folded up by a pulley and cord mechanism.

Stiff, tightly woven fabrics, such as heavier-grade cotton or linen, maintain a crisp edge along each fold; softer fabrics should be lined if they are to be considered for Roman shades.

Roman shades are usually professionally fabricated. Some manufacturers are beginning to offer premade Roman shades. Look for these where window treatments are sold, and install them according to manufacturer's instructions.

How a Roman Shade Works

The folds of a Roman shade are coordinated by a series of vertically attached tapes upon which rings are evenly spaced; cords are rigged through the rings. When the shade is raised, the cords are tethered to a cleat at the side of the window frame.

Balloon, Cloud, and Austrian Shades

A softer shade that takes advantage of filmier fabrics is the balloon. In a balloon shade, the outline of each individual, widely spaced

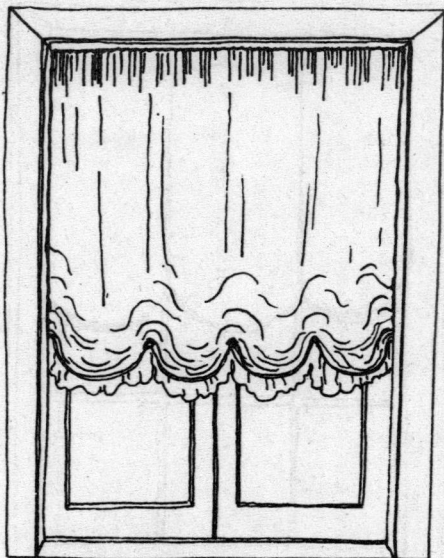

**Festoon Shade
with Ruffled Hem**

balloon panel is clearly defined. The balloon shade falls straight to a scalloped, slightly puffy hem.

The pouffier counterpart of the balloon, the cloud—or festoon—shade, falls loosely to its scalloped bottom hem; it has no defined panels. A third type of soft shade, the Austrian shade, is completely shirred, or gathered, from top to bottom, within each panel. Because of the shirring, Austrian shades must be made of even filmier fabric than balloons.

Honeycomb-Style Shades

One of the most recent introductions to the window shade market is the pleater shade and its variations, which are based on a honeycomb configuration. A simple pleater shade is just that, a shade

Balloon Shade

that accordion-folds on itself in pleats. The original pleater shades were fabricated of thick paper; now pleater shades are constructed of more durable, stiffened fabrics.

The honeycombs described above appear when the shade is lowered. The honeycomb pleater shade is actually double layered; when the shade drops, the layers separate and spread out into a series of open pleats. From the sides of the shades, the cavities between the layers (within the pleats) look like six-sided honeycomb cells.

One advantage to these shades is that they fold up and retreat inside a virtually invisible header. Once installed within or atop a window frame and raised completely, the shade is barely noticeable, except for its cord and cleat.

Honeycomb shades can be ordered in almost any color you can imagine. They may be textured, or pierced with tiny holes for a

more luminescent effect. Honeycombs are also available in specialized shapes; one of these is half-moon shaped to fit similarly
shaped windows called lunettes, which are generally installed over
standard windows to bring in extra light, and for architectural
interest.

Honeycombs, like roller shades, come with hardware and instructions for installation.

Mini- and Micro-Blinds

Besides roller shades, the easiest window treatment to buy ready-
made is the mini-blind. You can find minis in home centers and
decorating outlets, but also in paint and hardware stores. (A micro-
blind is distinguished from a mini-blind only by the width of its
slats—narrower, obviously, than a mini's.)

Mini-blinds come in a wide array of colors as well as metallic
tones. In the duplex configuration, their aluminum slats display
one color on the face and a different one at the back so that you
can effect two distinct looks at the window with a quick twist of
the slats. In hot climates, many people choose a reflective metallic
back to repel the glare and heat of the sun. Conversely, in cold
regions, a dark, heat-absorbent color may be selected.

If you opt for an inside installation—one within the casing—
subtract one-half inch from the width of your window so that there
is plenty of room to raise and lower the blind. The slats are
manipulated by a wand, or baton, that connects to a mechanism
inside the painted metal header. You can choose a left- or right-
hand placement of the wand. For convenience, it is best to relate
the wand to the placement of the window. If you have a pair of
side-by-side windows, it looks better if the left-hand window takes
a left-hand wand, the right, a right.

Installation instructions come with the shade; follow these.

Venetian Blinds

Venetian blinds—also called wooden blinds—are enjoying a re-
naissance after a period of virtual neglect. Crafted with 1", 2",
and even 3"-wide wood slats, venetian blinds are accented by
broad, thick cotton tapes that can be chosen in a color that har-
monizes with the overall decoration of a room. The color of the

wood is left up to you as well; choices vary from dark mahogany to light pine; slats may be painted instead of wood-stained.

Venetian blinds are usually installed by a professional.

Matchstick Blinds

A mainstay of many a college dorm and first apartment, matchstick blinds are an unbeatable choice when it comes to economy with style. Matchsticks can be trimmed at their edges to fit within or align with the outside edge of a window casing. They may be stained or painted, but are usually left natural. Matchsticks are slung within a pair of strings and roll up within the strings as they are raised. The pair of strings runs along the header, drops to one side, to be tethered to the window frame by a cleat or cup hook.

Vertical Blinds

Vertical blinds became immensely popular as an element in clean, spare, industrial-style rooms, and especially in rooms with large expanses of plate glass that looked burdened or overdone when covered any other way. Although that popularity has waned, they still work well, and are often installed as an antidote to clutter.

Vertical blinds are made with metal, stiffened fabric (often mesh), or plastic slats or blades that rotate to let in or shut out light and views. When pulled to one side, the slats take up very little room. The bottoms of the slats can be linked by thin chains to keep them steady.

Vertical blinds are usually used in ceiling-to-floor applications, but, if a band of windows sweeps across a wall or two above a sill (or heating unit or shelves), the blind will draw across the windowpanes only, and not drop to the floor.

Although verticals are most typically selected in white or metal tones, they can be purchased in colors, too. Like minis, they can display two tones, one on the face and one behind.

Verticals combine a wand and cord-and-pulley mechanism for ease of motion.

Vertical blinds are paired with a cornice. Vertical blind systems are usually installed by a professional.

Window Shutters

Interior shutters, usually outfitted with tilting louvres (or horizontal slats), are another "hard" alternative that afford even greater privacy than blinds or shades. Crafted of wood, shutters hinge and fold back against the window recess or jamb when not in use. When they are unfolded and the louvres closed, shutters cancel out virtually all light.

Shutters are usually installed in tiers, with one set of shutters protecting the lower half of the window, the other, the top half. This versatile arrangement allows the lower set to be closed for privacy while the upper set remains open to let in light.

Shutters come unfinished; it is up to you to seal and stain, or paint them if you so desire.

Installing Shutters

Shutters are fairly easy to install. First of all, measure the inside of your window casing and decide if you are going to use a single pair of shutters or two tiered pairs. (Remember, when you purchase shutters, allow for about ¼" to ½" between them so that they can close and lock easily. A bit of a gap between two shutters is better than a too-tight fit.)

Once you have brought your shutters home, hold a shutter in place and mark on the inside of the window casing where the hinges should be installed. Screw hinges onto the shutter first, and then screw the hinged shutter in place on the casing. Repeat with the rest of the shutters.

Plantation Shutters

The newest version of the shutter is actually not new at all. Based on traditional Southern-style prototypes, plantation shutters have wider louvres (up to 3" wide), and they usually are not installed in tiers. Rather, they are custom crafted to be tall enough to cover an entire window or even a French door. To allow a greater flow of air, especially tall shutters may be hinged in the middle so that the bottom half can tilt up and out; once the angle is set, the tilted portion of the shutter is held aloft by a long metal hook.

Windows bring in lots of light by day; daylight needs to be supplemented by artificial light in gloomy weather. In the next

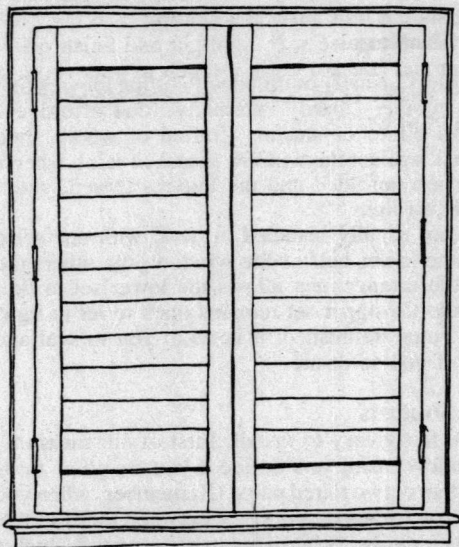

Plantation Shutters

chapter we turn to lighting, and to lamplight, as a way to dispel gloom and to light up the night as well.

To Recap

- Windows can be left unadorned or dressed, depending upon your need for privacy and how you want to have them complement your decorating scheme.
- Some windows are difficult to cover; look for specialty shades and hardware to solve the problem, if you want to cover them at all.
- Curtains tend to be informal and draperies formal partially because of fabric choices, and partially because of the hardware used in their installation. Drapery hardware is more complicated than the hardware used for curtains.
- Curtains are easy to make yourself, especially from sheets.

- Consider both the drop and the fullness of your window treatment; it should look lush, not skimpy.
- A valance or cornice will highlight and finish off a window treatment and add a decorator touch to your room scheme.
- Window shades or blinds can be used alone or paired with curtains or draperies.

CHAPTER 12

Lighting and Lamps

Lighting sets the mood of a room and affects the mood of its inhabitants more than any other single aspect of our homes. Just as it does in the theater, light will alter how a room looks and feels with a flick of a switch or the rotation of a rheostat or dimmer. When you move into a new house or apartment, a basic lighting system is in place, usually consisting of a series of overhead fixtures, outlets, and little else. This scheme allows you to see each room clearly, and it allows you to move throughout the spaces safely. A landlord or builder expects the tenant or home buyer to supply lamps or additional fixtures to supplement the basic lighting scheme.

To feel truly comfortable in a space, the lighting should comprise a balance from two or more of the following four sources—ambient light, activity or task light, atmospheric light, and accent light—which will not only establish an overall mood based on a balance between light and desired shadow, but will reflect your personal taste as well.

General or Ambient Light

General lighting is provided by overhead fixtures that are usually centered on the ceiling in each room. These fixtures illuminate the interior space. Brightness depends upon the bulb you select. Most people choose a 75 or 100 watt incandescent bulb or a fluorescent bulb that imparts the same amount of light. To augment the illumination, the overhead fixture is supplemented by a variety of additional fixtures such as wall sconces, portable floor and table lamps, and daylight.

Activity or Task Light

Many activities, such as reading, preparing foods, office work, and hobbies require a more intense, focused source of light. Table lamps, angled wall lights, track lighting, and pendants, which hang from the ceiling, target or pool light over a more concentrated area than ambient light. Focused light should be filtered or shielded to prevent glare and eyestrain.

The best bulbs for working are three-ways (the most common is a 50/100/150 incandescent), so you can control how much light you need, when you need it. The lowest setting, the 50-watt, is a mood light; the upper two settings are for short-term and long-term tasks. In other words, you should increase the brightness or intensity of the light with the increase in time required to complete the task.

Atmospheric Light

Some light fixtures are designed solely for mood, emitting light that usually is not bright enough to illuminate an activity. Atmospheric light fixtures may be consciously sculptural; an example of these are artfully shaped wall sconces. Atmosphere can also be elicited by dimmers controlling the intensity of light from a chandelier, for instance, or from table lamps.

Art or Accent Light

Small spotlights used to target paintings, sculpture, or even plants are called accent lights. These concentrate their beam solely on the work of art. Other sources of light, such as candles, are also considered accent lights. All of these typically complement or supplement a general source of light. Employed totally on their own, they can be considered atmospheric.

Lighting Zones

Lighting essentially maps out three zones or latitudes within a room—the areas above, at, and below eye level. The level above is, obviously, the one controlled by the ambient lighting emanating from the ceiling fixture. This zone may be enhanced by moldings installed with soft lighting behind them. A cornice runs along the ceiling line and directs light down the wall; a cove, set a few inches below the ceiling line, directs light upward toward and across the ceiling.

The zone at eye level, dominated by freestanding floor lamps and table lamps, encompasses the work or activity areas; because of the intensity of light required for most tasks, the mid-zone tends to be the brightest. The zone below eye level is one that needs little light; here accent lights predominate, such as floor spots for highlighting plants.

What Light Is Best?

In rooms with combined activities, or rooms that are both public and private—such as a library or guest bedroom—light should be balanced from at least two lighting sources, ambient and activity. Accent or atmospheric lighting can be rheostated from these or added separately.

If you want to eliminate a ceiling fixture, be sure you generate enough ambient light from other sources, such as wall sconces or floor and table lamps with translucent shades for maximum diffusion. Keep a light on when you watch television to avoid eyestrain.

Installing Lighting

Because of the risk of electrocution, it is safest to have lighting that is to be mounted on the ceiling or wall installed by a professional electrician who can make the necessary hookups.

Light for Entertaining

Rooms that are the scene of a great deal of entertaining should take advantage of atmospheric light. Such rooms tend to be less concerned with individual or solitary activities such as reading or sewing. You should place one or a pair of lamps strategically on the surface you will use for serving foods or cocktails (or install recessed lights in the ceiling instead), but otherwise, you can simply complement the ambient light with dimmers and accent lights—and candles or hurricane lamps.

Reading Light

The light that must be calibrated most for comfort is activity or task light, and especially light to read by. The best light for reading combines diffused ambient light with a stronger concentration of light on the surface of your book or other reading material.

A floor or table lamp with a translucent shade that is at least 16″ in diameter at the base is a good solution because the shade filters enough ambient light for comfort while the lamp itself provides the light. A shaded lamp should be positioned so that the bottom of the shade is level with your eye; usually about 40″ to 42″ from the floor.

A table lamp should stand about 20″ away from the center of your book, and slightly behind you (preferably at your shoulder), to avoid glare; a floor lamp should stand a bit farther away, about 26″ behind the center of your book.

Reading in Bed

Bedrooms should combine good reading light near the bed with a pleasant, perhaps romantic overall radiance. Bedside lamps may

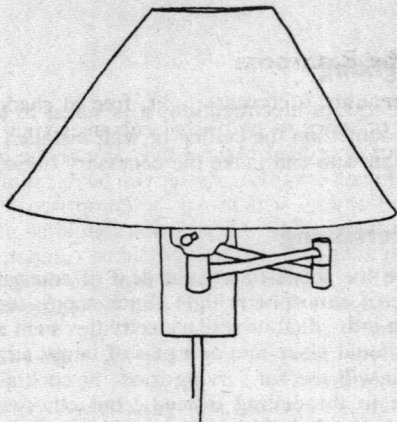

Swing-Arm Lamp

be affixed to the wall or may stand on tables. The most versatile bedside lamp is a wall-hung swing-arm with a translucent shade because you can control its lateral position for reading comfort. If you purchase a swing-arm lamp, ask for a matching metal strip to cover the exposed portion of the cord.

As mentioned previously, unless you are comfortable with the idea of hooking up electrical wires, it is best to ask a professional to install a wall lamp such as a swing-arm. If you are renting your place, your superintendent or handyman might be able to do this for you.

Other Bedroom Lighting
If you have a dressing table in your bedroom, place a pair of small lamps on either side of the table so that you will achieve an even glow across your face while grooming. Closet or wardrobes should be adequately lit to aid in dressing.

In children's bedrooms—as throughout the house—open outlets should be plugged with safety shields to prevent children from sticking something into the socket.

A child needs a good reading light, light to play by, and perhaps even a night-light to dispel fear.

Lighting the Bathroom

Grooming requires a constant light, free of shadows, preferably from a pair or series of bulbs that enhances your complexion. A lighted mirror or special fixtures may already be installed in your baths; if you want to replace these, you have a number of choices. One is strip lighting, which may be comprised of makeup bulbs on a strip or with tubing. These strips should be placed 30" apart, one on either side of a mirrored medicine cabinet, to avoid glare. Another choice is to place a single strip over the cabinet. As stated previously, it is best to have lighting professionally installed for safety reasons.

Whatever your choice, use flattering soft white or soft pink bulbs in the fixture.

If your bath is large and you think it will get cold during the winter months, you may want to add a recessed infrared heat lamp to the lighting lineup. This heat lamp can be installed next to or near the ceiling fixture. An infrared lamp gives off minimal light, so it cannot replace an existing fixture.

While you are at it, you might consider putting in a ventilating fan if your bathroom has no window or other ready source of ventilation. A ventilating fan prevents a buildup of moisture in the room and thus prevents mildew.

Lighting the Kitchen

The kitchen presents a special case, because you will want ambient light for overall illumination, but each work zone should be highlighted as well as each countertop.

The kitchen typically comprises two distinct areas, the actual work triangle reaching from stove to sink to refrigerator, and the eating area. A pendant lamp can hang over a breakfast table (allow a 30" clearance so you don't bump your head); others may be suspended over a work island. It is a good idea to light the stove and the sink, too. This can be accomplished with a recessed light or two, with a track setup, or, over the sink, with a strip hidden behind a valance over the window, if you have one.

All of these fixtures should be installed by a professional electrician.

Lighting Countertops

To light countertops located under banks of wall cabinets, the easiest solution is to install under-cabinet fluorescent strips (these run from one foot to four feet in length), shielded by a strip of wood called a lambrequin to prevent glare. These strips should be mounted as close to the front of the cabinets as possible, and each should measure at least two-thirds the length of the countertop below it.

Under cabinet strips need not be professionally installed; most are packaged with sticky-backed mounts or with mounting brackets or clips. Figure out where you want to hang your strip, mark the spot, install the mounts, and affix the strip. The strip comes with a cord and plug, like a lamp, so it can be plugged into a convenient outlet.

Hallways and Stairs

These should be adequately lighted, primarily for safety reasons, but also to complement adjoining rooms. Ceiling fixtures and/or wall sconces should do the trick, as long as switch plates and stair treads are clear to view. If you hang art or photographs, you might want to consider adding special accent fixtures that attach to or install over each work of art.

The Entry and Outdoor Lighting

Do you want to dramatize your entry, or is it just a place to shed outerwear and store boots, umbrellas, and other paraphernalia? How you utilize your entry will dictate the kind of lighting to use. Three options to consider are a small chandelier, recessed lighting, or a couple of wall sconces. Again, for safety, you want to be able to clearly reach and see the switch plate upon entry, just as you do in halls and stairwells.

If you have a house or garden apartment or condominium, you should make certain the lighting surrounding your front door ensures your safe arrival home, as well as welcomes guests. A pair of outdoor lanterns elevated 66″ off the ground on either side of the front door provides adequate illumination, as does one single lamp suspended from an overhang, porch, or vestibule ceiling.

If you have a front yard or walkway, be sure lighting leading up to the front door is adequate, too.

The professional electrician will make sure that your outdoor lighting is protected from moisture, especially hard-driving rain. Protection is usually afforded by waterproof caulking.

Decorating with Lamps

A decorating scheme is incomplete without lighting, and—for most of us—without lamps. Yet few people consider lamps as more than decorative accessories, to purchase at whim and place wherever some localized lighting might be needed.

Deliberating your lighting needs in terms of activities or mood, as outlined above, should give you a better idea about the kinds of lamps you may want to complement your lifestyle. Remember, though, that lighting and lamps also function as an integral part of the decor.

When to Buy Lamps

Lamps can visually make or break a room. Their height and bulk, proportion, scale, and style affect the balance of a furniture arrangement. You should select your lamps—especially your table lamps—**after** your decide on your furniture, if you can, so that you can plan for a harmonious effect. If you cannot, it is best to purchase lamps that are not too highly stylized, nor too tall.

Choosing a Table Lamp

Ideally, any lamp—be it a floor lamp or a table lamp—should stand so that its bulb is located 40″ to 42″ off the floor, with the bottom of the shade aligned with your eye. Depending upon the height of a table, the best height for a table lamp is between 22″ and 28″ tall. If the shade is too high, the bulb will shine in your eyes; if the shade is too low, the light will not fall on your lap or book.

The tables that flank a sofa or stand next to a chair look most balanced when they measure either 2″ higher or lower than the arm of the sofa or chair. If a table is much higher or lower, it will look out of sync. It is also inconvenient to reach for an object on the table when it is too high or too low.

The height of the table, therefore, will dictate the height of the

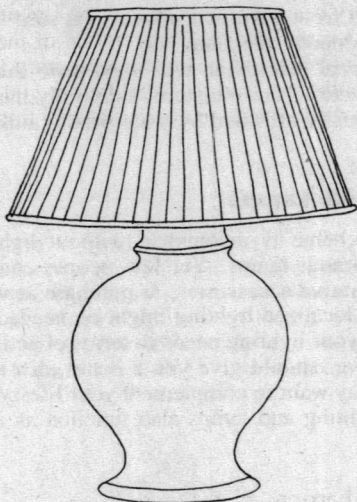

**Ginger Jar Lamp
with Pleated Shade**

lamp upon it. If the table is 2″ higher than the arm of the sofa, then the lamp should be shorter than if the table is 2″ shorter than the arm.

Kinds of Table Lamps

A table lamp can be made from almost anything, it seems. Many fine lamps, both antique and contemporary, are based on or converted from other decorative accessories such as vases, urns, even wooden spools and boxes or fat tin cans. Lamps are made from a wide range of materials, including metals such as brass, wrought iron or tin, crystal, porcelain, wood, and even wire and paper.

Traditionally, lamps were assembled or designed to coordinate with furniture groupings. In some instances, lamps—like mirrors—were highly valued and coveted as fashion items. Many very early lamps replicated their forerunners, candlesticks. Others were converted from porcelains that were imported from abroad; the Chinese ginger jar is an example of this type. Today, both the candlestick lamp and the ginger jar are still considered classics.

Contemporary designer lamps tend to be sinuous and sculptural and often slender, and are typically crafted of metal that is either burnished or painted black. Many contemporary lamps only work with halogen bulbs, so read the label before you make your purchase (we will discuss halogen bulbs later in this chapter).

The Architect's Lamp

Another contemporary lamp that retains its popularity is the architect's lamp. With its serviceable rotating factory-style shade and adjustable, pivoting arm, this lamp is eminently versatile, especially for home offices and children's rooms. The architect's lamp is available with a screw-on weighted base or with a clamp; the clamp allows it to be attached to a bookcase or other vertical support, as well as to a table (without a rim or apron) or shelf.

One popular variation on the architect's lamp is the Tizio, named

**Candlestick Lamp with
Firm Pleated Shade**

by its designer. Because it is a designer lamp, the Tizio is quite expensive. The Tizio takes a halogen bulb, but otherwise pivots and bends just like an architect's lamp.

Floor Lamps

Although they seem more cumbersome than table lamps, floor lamps are more portable because they can be shifted and adjusted without altering a tabletop scheme. Some floor lamps purposely are skirted with shelves or tables so that they combine the attributes of both. This type of lamp/table works well in many instances because the bulb is already positioned at the correct height for reading or other armchair activities.

POPULAR FLOOR LAMPS

Pharmacy lamps	Copies of those used in pharmacies in the early part of this century. Made of brass or chrome, with a long pipelike stem connecting a weighted base and shade. They vary in style according to their shades: the classic triangular **tent** shade, the round **bubble** shade, and the **shell,** which looks like a scallop shell. The stand adjusts up and down to eliminate glare from the bulb. The shade swivels to beam light in any direction.
Torchiere	Designed to direct light up and away, toward the ceiling. Functions best for atmosphere or to supplement ambient lighting.

Lampshades

You can find lampshades in specialty stores, department stores, and even five and dime stores. The most expensive shades are made out of silk. Durable copies are made of a less costly fabric, such as rayon. Ready-made fabric shades are offered in white or ivory or ecru, neutral shades that go with virtually any decorating scheme. If you like, you can custom order a fabric shade in a color, but most colors will dull or inhibit lamplight. Shades can also be made of paper or metal.

Shape and Proportion

No matter what the material, it is the shape, scale, and proportion of the shade that matters most. You do not want a shade that looks

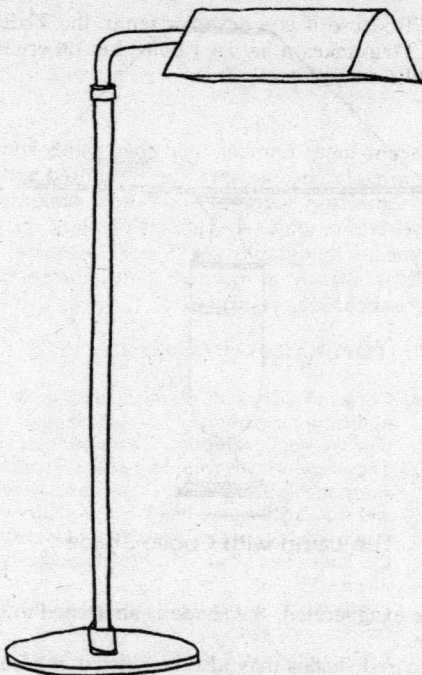

**Pharmacy Lamp
with Tent Shade**

top-heavy, nor do you want a shade that exposes the bulb or its socket. Unless the lamp is very tall and narrow, like a candlestick, chances are that the most harmonious shade, one that will most suit a standard base, will be almost equal in height to the base, and about 16″ across the bottom rim for maximum diffusion of light. Examples: the ginger jar and the canister, which is a cylindrical base made of porcelain or metal. In both of these cases, the shade is about the same height as the base.

Shade Styles
Most shades are slightly tapered with an opening at the top that is almost equal in diameter as that at the bottom. As the taper

Urn Lamp with Coolie Shade

becomes more exaggerated, the shade is shortened to counterbalance the taper.

Standard tapered shades may also be shirred or pleated to give them a richness of texture.

Coolie   Named for their similarity to this Chinese headgear. Looks best on tall, slender lamps such as candlesticks.

Pagoda   Has faceted sides and a flared bottom rim. Often teams up with thick columnar lamps, with lamps with vase- or urn-inspired bases, and canister bases.

Tapered   Generic term; shade may be circular, oval, or faceted. Ovals look best on lamps with a double- or multiple-column base.

Tent   Tapered rectangular shade.

Purchasing a Shade

Lampshades are available in a variety of constructions to fit specific types of lamps. Does your lamp have a harp, which is the metal frame surrounding the bulb, and a socket—or just a socket, which is the metal part that the bulb screws into? If it has only a socket, does it require a shade that twists onto the socket, or a shade that clamps onto the light bulb? Most table lamps are fitted with a harp; many floor lamps and wall lamps are not. Check yours.

If you are purchasing a shade for a table lamp separately from its base, it is a good idea to take the base in and consult the salesperson regarding the most appropriate shade. If you cannot transport the lamp, take in a photograph of it, with its measurements jotted on the back, to work from.

Decorative Options

Once you have decided on the size and shape of your shade, you have some other options to consider. Would you like a pleated shade or one that is gathered or shirred? Do you want to embellish your shade, be it fabric or paper, with trimming? Would you like your shades to be stenciled or pierced with cutouts?

Do you want to have your shades covered with fabric to match or coordinate with the fabric used on your sofa, pillows, or window treatments? Some furniture manufacturers offer lamps and shades that coordinate with their furnishings; otherwise an interior decorator or a home-furnishings or specialty shop can fabricate shades to your exact specifications.

Cover a Paper Shade with Fabric

If you are handy, you can make your own fabric-covered shade using a paper shade as a form. If the shade is tapered, as most are, you will have to cut your fabric so that it fits around the bottom rim and correct with gentle darts.

Cut the fabric so that it will completely encircle the shade, and so that it will be able to be folded, like a hem, over the top and bottom of the shade.

Spray fabric adhesive to the back of the fabric. Press the fabric over the shade, adjusting for darts. Darts are like little triangular pleats. As you work your way around the shade, pleat the darts as you go, wherever they seem appropriate to correct the fit. It looks best, of course, if they are evenly spaced. As you work your way around, make sure there are no air bubbles or wrinkles, either.

Finally, if you like, run a compatible trim, such as seam binding or ribbon, around the top and bottom, both inside and out to cover the raw edges.

Controlling Light

No matter what your light source, you can install rheostats or dimmers to control the intensity of light for any given situation. Most dimmers are installed instead of standard switch plates; the most sophisticated of these reacts to touch, registering intensity levels on a readout. Others slide or rotate, some with push buttons that turn the light on and off or return it to the previous lighting level.

Types of Bulbs

The bulb (also called a *lamp* by professionals, which can be confusing) that you choose can affect the quality of light. There are basically three types of bulbs: incandescent (the most commonplace, called general-service bulbs) and reflectors, tungsten-halogen (which is a type of incandescent), and fluorescent. Of the three, fluorescents are by far the most energy efficient, consuming only one-fifth the electricity needed to power incandescents. Fluorescents last up to twenty times longer, too.

Unfortunately, fluorescents garnered a bad reputation because what we think of as the typical fluorescent bulb emitted a greenish glow that was not attractive to humans or foods. Today, though, manufacturers offer a wide spectrum of whites (and some colors), including daylight and warm white, which emulates the white emitted by an incandescent. Fluorescents also now come in a variety of bulb shapes besides the traditional straight tube, so they can be used in table and floor lamps as well as in ceiling or undercabinet fixtures. The most useful is a screw-in bulb that fits into any standard lamp socket.

Specialty Bulbs

Because reflector bulbs have a silvery coating inside the bulb, their light is directed and concentrated more than that diffused by a standard incandescent. Reflectors are available in two versions: floodlights, which spread the light, and spotlights which target their beam. Because of its controlled beam, reflectors are often used in track lighting.

Halogen Bulbs

Tungsten-halogen bulbs present an intensely bright, white light that is more powerful than that given off by a standard incandescent. Halogens last longer, but they are fragile and require special handling. The glass sheathing the bulb should not be touched by bare fingers because it has a special coating on it that reacts adversely to body oils and sweat. Low-voltage halogens also require a transformer to correct, or step down, the voltage.

Despite this inconvenience, halogens—especially the low-voltage versions—are becoming increasingly popular, in part because they have radically affected lamp design. Because halogen bulbs tend to be miniaturized, the lamps they complement can be smaller, slighter, and more delicate in profile. Halogen lamps take up less room on a table or desk; hanging lamps are more slender— less of a visual obstruction.

Halogen bulbs are most often used in place of reflectors; many halogens mimic reflectors in their shape—but in miniature. The smallest halogen is called a bipin or peanut and is used in desk lamps as well as small tracks.

Lamps as Accessories

Even though lamps are practical, they are also considered the prime accessory in a decorating scheme. They should fit in with other accessories, complement them, and light them as well. In turn, accessories should look and feel comfortable in the company of lamps. In our concluding chapter, we will look briefly at accessories. Our look will be brief because accessories are the most personal of belongings, and a book such as this cannot—and should not—dictate what feels personal to you.

To Recap

- Lighting is generated by four sources: ambient or general lighting, activity lighting to target tasks, atmospheric lighting to enhance mood, and accent lighting to pinpoint specific objects.
- Balance two or more of these light sources to make a room feel comfortable.

- Reading lights and lamps should be positioned properly on the table, wall, or floor to prevent glare from the bulb from getting in your eyes.
- Adequate lighting is important for safety reasons, too.
- To fit into a decorating scheme, lamps should be appropriate to the situation and setting.
- Lampshades and bulbs will affect the quality of light.

CHAPTER 13

Accessories

Everything you add to your basic decorating scheme, to accent the scheme and infuse it with your special touch and taste, is an important clue to how you live. Accessories tell more about personality and about how comfortable a home feels than any other single element. The instinct to collect and to accessorize—to mark a place with our personality—is strong and deep. Photographs, books, collections, even plants and flowers, are all highly idiosyncratic; they speak volumes about their owners.

Calm versus Clutter

Some people live in spartan settings, with few extraneous possessions. In rooms such as these, each and every accessory—from a lamp, to a vase, to a candle, to a painting or statue—seems to stand out and apart from its surroundings. Juxtaposition of ele-

179

ments is key to a spare decor. How large or diminutive each piece is in relation to the rest of the room's furnishings tells a great deal about how the owners of the rooms feel about proportion, scale, and harmony. Each piece, indeed, seems invested with a special aura all its own, an aura that combines drama and calm.

By contrast, highly cluttered rooms blend belongings with background to create a more invigorating atmosphere. Too many possessions, of course, serve to stifle a room, but clusters of well-chosen objects can appear simultaneously stimulating and cozy.

Choosing Accessories

Over the course of time, we accumulate possessions: many are things we acquire because we need them. Some of our possessions, though, are things we buy because they strike our fancy. Some people have an uncanny and unerring awareness of what they like and don't like. They are drawn to a particular collectible, for instance, and make a point of showcasing it in all its variety and glory. Others acquire myriad things, from their families, from travels, or some simply from an urge to nest.

Where Accessories Come From
Anything that is portable, personal, and empowered with meaning can be considered an accessory. The list of potential accessories is endless—from cast-offs to curios, from candlesticks to counterpanes, from crafts to coin collections—and so, therefore, is the list of places where they can be found: your grandmother's attic; flea markets, garage sales, and auctions; shops specializing in home furnishings or antiques; even the roadside, woods, and beach.

Often the accessories we love the most are discovered in unexpected places and unexpected ways. That is one reason why mementos are so evocative; like souvenirs, they conjure up memories and connect us to places, occasions, and people.

Rules for Displaying Accessories

There are few rules for display. These are basically the same as those that govern good design: proportion, balance, scale, and harmony. All come into play when a group of objects is agreeably arranged. If objects are gathered helter-skelter, then they will look and feel out of kilter.

Objects on a Tabletop

On a tabletop, for example, an interplay of tall and squat items— a ginger jar lamp, say, with a short stack of books, framed photographs, a small vase of flowers and perhaps a bowl or votive candle or two—offers a mix that is pleasing to the eye. No single item dominates; all contribute equally to the "tablescape."

That same tablescape, of course, should not be written in stone. Things should be able to be moved about or taken away or replaced. The main rule, if it is a rule, is that the tabletop look comfortable, not overwhelmed.

Organizing Yourself

Display is as much a sense of organization as a sense of placement or position. Where do you want to display any single object or group of objects? On a shelf or shelves? On tabletops or the tops of chests or bureaus? On the wall?

The main thing to consider is how to separate and divide up your possessions. When you think about what should go where, you should not overlook the matter of convenience. Will it be easy, for example, to dust a collection of figurines if it is placed on a high shelf in an open cupboard? Will it be easy to access a book once it has been allotted its spot in a bookcase, or sandwiched in a stack on the floor or coffee table? Can you find that CD when you want to play it for friends?

An Eye Level Rule

It is best to relate your largest accessories to your eye level while you are seated; first of all, you want to be able to see most of your things without tilting your head too far back. If large objects or paintings are placed too high, they will appear top-heavy and look as if they will topple forward.

Thus, it is best to hang a painting or group of artwork quite close to the top of a sofa, and not near the ceiling. If the painting is positioned in such a manner, it will relate to the furnishings; if it is placed too high, it will appear to float on the wall in a disconnected way.

Large objects, such as vases full of flowers or pieces of sculpture, baskets filled with yarn or needlework, or big coffee table books should be placed on a tabletop or on a low stool or pedestal (or even on the floor) and not on a high shelf. Because of their size, they seem to naturally anchor a setting. If they are placed too high, they will look as if they are crushing the room.

A Case for Symmetry

A pair of objects, such as candlesticks, look well when they flank another, centrally positioned object. On a wall, pairs of plates ascending on either side of a painting or platter over a sideboard, or a pair of sconces bracketing a mirror in an entryway appear harmonious and in balance. Make sure the central object relates to eye level; its companions can be adjusted higher or lower depending upon the furniture in the scheme.

Hanging Pictures

The case for eye level viewing applies strongly to paintings, as mentioned previously, as well as to posters and other artwork or photographs. Most people hang pictures too high, which strains the point of view. Pictures should be enjoyed while the viewer is seated, so lowering the position of any wall art is a boon to their appreciation.

Before hanging pictures, especially a group or cluster of pictures, it is best to lay them out on the floor first. Pretending that the floor is a wall, you can shift the pictures around until they comprise a pleasing arrangement. Hang the central picture first, adjusting it to eye level, and then compose the rest according to your floor plan.

When you hang pictures, too, keep adjoining walls in mind, so that the room overall will retain a sense of balance. For example, you may want to spread your pictures across all four walls rather than group them all on one. If you have two large pictures, they may look best facing each other across a room.

Positioning on Shelves

When arranging objects on shelves, the general rule of thumb is to place less-used objects out of reach and most-used ones within reach. A sense of scale comes into play, however, if such objects are open to view. Bulky objects are best enjoyed at or below eye level—or they should be stored out of sight.

Balancing Objects

When you cluster objects in a shelving system, place large items at the back, smaller items in front. For balance, a large item should center the collection, with smaller items ranging to either side.

Individual objects, such as small pieces of folk art, plates up-ended on plate easels, vases, or other sculptural items, can set off and break up, as well as highlight, rows of books.

Books

Books can assume a variety of poses; they may be ranked upright, stacked, or tilted just so into or against an accommodating book-end—or all of the above simultaneously. Sometimes it is easier to lay overscaled books on their sides; one advantage of this, too, is that their titles are effortlessly read.

Large books should be relegated to low shelves; they, too, can appear top-heavy if they are stored above eye level, and it is easier to pull them out if they are on lower shelves.

Encountering Electronics

As technology becomes more and more sophisticated, more and more of the things we live with—and find necessary to our well-being—are governed by electronics. Home entertainment systems (including stereo, television, videocassette player), computers, telephones, photocopiers, fax machines, video games and other electronic toys, radios, and clocks are all items few of us could live without as we head into the twenty-first century.

Electronics are finally being designed to blend in with a decorating scheme rather than defiantly fight it. Streamlining and a reliance on monotonal blacks and metallics allow most electronics to merge unostentatiously with their surroundings. And casings have been developed to consolidate dangling wires.

Home Entertainment Centers

Housing this plethora of equipment taxes our ingenuity and our sense of design. Luckily, furniture systems called home entertainment centers are available to house clusters of components. These centers combine cabinets fitted with doors and with open bookshelves so that each individual component can be easily accessed.

Accessorizing the Home Office

With more and more people working from home, setting up space for a computer and auxiliary equipment has come to the forefront of home design. Keeping accessories personal at the same time as they organize office gear allows a home office to become an unobtrusive part of a comfortable decorating scheme.

Wooden file cabinets that look like side tables with deep drawers replace the standard metal files, and computer desks may mimic eighteenth-century furniture designs.

On top of the desk, low baskets and bins, pencil trays, and attractive table lamps all combine to look homey rather than clinical and off-putting. Photographs and favorite works of art or a discreetly displayed collection of books or objects help integrate the office setup into its surroundings.

A Last Word: Your Accessories Are You

In the final analysis, what items you choose to live with and how you choose to live with them is a testament to **how** you want to live. Accessories complement furnishings; both complement you. Of all the elements in your home, you are the ultimate, and most important, accessory—you and those you love having around you.

To Recap

- Accessories are the personal touches that define a home and its owner; they also define the mood of a room.
- Organization is key to a harmonious display of objects.
- To keep a room in balance, accessories should relate to your eye level while seated; objects or paintings on the walls or in shelves should be placed so that they do not appear top-heavy.

- Arrange home electronics and home office equipment for ease of access.
- Last, but not least, remember that you and those you share your home with are the most important accessories of all. If you and they are comfortable, then your home will feel comfortable, too.